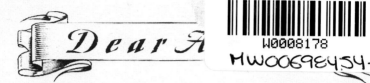

Dear A...

Standing in the Light

The Captive Diary of Catharine Carey Logan

BY MARY POPE OSBORNE

Scholastic Inc.   New York

Delaware Valley, Pennsylvania
1763

13th of Eleventh Month, 1763

Today Papa gave Thomas and me new copybooks, black-walnut ink, and quills. I shall use mine for a diary, as well as for schoolwork.

The house is still. I write in the loft by candlelight while Thomas and Eliza sleep near me.

Papa is snoring downstairs. Mother sings softly in the dark to Baby Will. He suffers from his first tooth.

Mother shed a tear of joy when she discovered this tooth, for her last two babies did not live long enough to have one. She always worries about Baby Will. Weeks ago he was just skin and bone after a bout of fever and diarrhea. But lately she says again and again: "My, Baby Will has grown fatter, dost thee not all agree?"

We start school again tomorrow after helping bring in the harvest. I am so excited I can barely sleep. I confess I am looking forward to seeing Jess Owen. I have many things to tell him.

14th of Eleventh Month, 1763

All in the girls' school were talking about Jess Owen today. He has returned to the boys' school next door after spending six months away in Philadelphia. He has grown much taller and appears to be the most handsome boy in the valley.

Last winter, Jess and I were good friends. I talked easily to him and teased him. But today I was shocked to learn that I felt exceedingly shy when I first saw him on the path through the sugar maple grove.

He waved to me and called my name. The sun was bright on the maples, and a gentle breeze blew, making the last leaves fall around him like yellow stars.

I only nodded in return, then walked more quickly, for I was in a flutter.

When Thomas asked why I was walking so fast, I hushed him. In truth, I suddenly did not know what I would say if Jess were to walk with us.

I am confused now about my attack of fear. I pray I will soon find my tongue.

15th of Eleventh Month, 1763

Weather unusually warm. Papa burned trees yesterday, and the air is still sweet with the smell of burnt wood.

Before school, Thomas and I caught the pigs eating pumpkins and we chased them with sticks. When Thomas struck one, Mother saw him and severely told him to exert himself with more loving-kindness.

Thomas protested, for he is seven years old and does not like to have his will crossed.

Mother told him to watch his impudent tongue. She said that God loves all His creatures, however humble.

"Even naughty pigs?" Thomas asked with his usual mischievous grin.

"Yes, and even naughty boys," Mother said.

If God loves all His creatures, I pray He will have mercy on *me* and untie my tongue.

16th of Eleventh Month, 1763

Unpleasant news from Master Collins today: Soon Lucy, Molly, and I must learn how to divide the long numbers. I fear I shall never understand and shall be afraid even to ask questions. I pray to be more courageous both in matters concerning arithmetic and talking to boys such as Jess Owen.

17th of Eleventh Month, 1763

Monthly Meeting today. The Friends disowned Sarah Thompson for dancing and singing, John Palmer for buying a slave, Ezekiel Carter for enlisting in the army, Liza Bennet for deviating from plainness of dress, Rebecca Merrick for marrying one not of our religious society, and Elizabeth Knowlton for having a vain and airy manner. Christopher Betts acknowledged it was shameful for him to ride in a horse race and to play cards.

Then, in the silence, I found myself thinking about Jess Owen waving at me in the grove.

What has happened to the girl I was last year? The spirited girl who spoke to Jess so easily? Was she too bold? Was her manner too vain and airy? Would the Friends eventually turn out that girl? I fear she was not very modest and courteous, as the Quakers require a young woman to be. Sometimes alone in the woods, she even danced and sang!

But I confess I miss her. She was a happy creature.

18th of Eleventh Month, 1763

Before Jess Owen left the schoolyard today, his eyes seemed to seek me out. Then he waved and called my name.

Molly and Lucy both saw his action. Molly marveled that Jess Owen had called to me — and that I was red in the face.

Her words frighten me. I feel that my face betrayed me — revealing my strong feelings for Jess! I must find a way to hide myself so no one can guess what I think or feel.

19th of Eleventh Month, 1763

Mother boiled potatoes tonight. We mashed them with milk and butter, then cooked them in the skillet and served them with honey. A better pancake dinner was never had. The whole family cheerful and thankful, except me. I was in an inexplicably gloomy mood. Mother scolded me for looking cross.

But then Papa invited me to go out into the night with him and look through his spyglass at the stars. They are so plentiful tonight, they moved Papa to quote Scripture: "When I consider Thy heavens, the work of Thy fingers, the moon and stars, each Thou hast ordained. What is man, that Thou art mindful of him?"

I wish I had the courage to talk to Jess Owen about Papa's spyglass. But I worry now that whatever I say will sound too vain or too airy. I think I should say only simple things: "How was thy time in Philadelphia, Jess? How dost thee like returning to our school?"

21st of Eleventh Month, 1763

Anxious day. Stayed home, as Baby Will is unwell. He had a fever and diarrhea again, so severe that Papa left off farming and went for Doctor Griffith.

By noon the doctor arrived and diagnosed that Baby Will has worms. He fed him rhubarb and pinkroot. Finally the baby slept peacefully in Mother's arms.

For the rest of the day, I tended to Eliza and the cooking, sweeping, feeding livestock, and collecting eggs.

Dear God, please keep Baby Will under Thy wing.

22nd of Eleventh Month, 1763

Plain and simple day.

Thomas and I stayed home to help Mother again. Baby Will seems to be conquering his worms. Mother, in a cheerful mood, made stewed apples and sweet biscuits for breakfast.

It was gray and windy as Thomas and I carried six buckets each from the spring and Eliza collected kindling. We filled the great iron pot over the fire and heated the water, then scrubbed a week's worth of dirty clothes. While we worked, I made Thomas recite his multiplication tables and spelling words.

Later I gave Eliza a quilting lesson while Thomas practiced his penmanship. He can write with a joining hand and make capitals now.

In the afternoon Mother made candles while I took Eliza and Thomas into the forest to gather nuts. Thomas tore his britches climbing a tree in quest of a bird's nest and Eliza cried because her stomach was hurting. I fear she might have worms, too.

Though she is four years old, she is quite small, so I was able to carry her all the way home. Mother gave her rhubarb and pinkroot. Then I baked johnnycakes and boiled turnips for Thomas and Papa.

23rd of Eleventh Month, 1763

Papa was gone all day, comforting the Lancasters who have recently lost two children to whooping cough.

When he returned, we had devotions and prayed for the souls of the children. Then Papa showed us tiny wildflowers he had found on his journey. Somehow they have survived all the early frosts.

Thomas asked Papa why he bothered with such tiny things.

Papa said that we must study *all* the things of our world because no matter how small, each wears the mark of our Maker.

This thought gives new meaning to the owl that hoots in the dark, my leaping candle flame, the whispery breathing sounds of Baby Will downstairs.

Perhaps God hoots. God leaps. And God breathes downstairs.

These are the thoughts I should like to share with Jess Owen.

24th of Eleventh Month, 1763

Eliza seems better. Mama even allowed her to go with all of us to the Meeting House.

As we sat in silence, ill-behaved boys in the gallery laughed once during worship. I fear I heard the laughter of Jess Owen among them.

After Meeting, Mother called them "impudent children," loud enough for them to hear. (Oh, how mistaken to call *Jess* a child!)

Mother keeps a list for her children on how to behave at Meeting. I know it by heart:

> No talking, laughing, biting nails, pinching neighbors, stretching, yawning, spitting, staring at others, tapping of feet, or sighs of impatience.

Often it seems impossible to sit for two hours without succumbing to at least one of these temptations.

When I walked by Jess on the way to our carriage, he smiled at me — in front of all!

I looked away, blushing red in the face.

Mother might say that he has a wild character because he plays pinch-penny and laughs in Meeting. 'Tis strange that I do not care. I fear that in my deepest heart, I am a bit of a wild creature myself.

26th of Eleventh Month, 1763

Great distress. Jess Owen caught up with me on the path to school and, in the most beguiling voice, asked me if I liked blue ribbons.

I asked him why he wanted to know, and he answered that he thought I would look very pretty with blue ribbons in my hair.

I prayed for composure . . . and all I received was this inspiration: "Watch thy impudent tongue, Jess Owen."

What a *horrible* thing to say! It sounds like what Mother would say! I could die a thousand deaths for having spoken thus!

Jess smiled a bit of a smirk and walked away. I wished I could walk away from myself as well.

So I would say this was a most miserable day. My face grows hot just to remember my words.

27th of Eleventh Month, 1763

I was relieved to stay home today and help Mother, for I did not have to face Jess Owen. However, I am sad that Eliza is unwell again. Her stomachache came back before dawn, so all morning Mother rocked her while I tended Baby Will.

When Papa came in from working in the fields, he fetched Doctor Griffith, who treated Eliza with red bark. Soon she slept soundly and without pain.

I fear Mother and I were greatly alarmed by news the doctor brought. He reported that Indians have raided three farmhouses on the river. Mother clutched me and, nearly in tears, exclaimed, "What terrible news!" She is very frightened of the Indians. I fear I could offer her little comfort, for my own heart was beating with fear.

Papa spoke to her in a calm, soft voice saying that we should put our trust in God. I wanted to believe him, but when he saw the doctor out to his carriage, I rushed after him. I waited until the doctor had driven away, then said, "What dost thee truly think about the Indian attack?"

"I expected as much," he answered.

He stopped to sit on a log and motioned for me to sit with him. He explained that our government had lied to the Indians and broken all its treaties with them. Now the English were refusing to leave the Indian territories, even though our war with the French has ended.

He also told me how the Indians had been cruelly betrayed by the Extravagant Day's Walk. Years ago, the Delaware Indians had agreed that the English could have all the land that they could walk in one and a half days. Both sides understood that to be thirty miles. Before the official walk, however, the English cheated by cutting a path through the virgin forest. Then they hired expert runners to race over the path. So the English ended up with twice the land they deserved.

"If we treat the Indians fairly, they will treat us fairly!" Papa said. "For forty years after William Penn came here, there was not one death on either side. But then the white men lied to the Indians and used them as pawns in the land wars between the French and English. The French convinced them to fight on their side by telling them that the English were planning to make them slaves."

I am sad for the Indians, but I confess I worry more about our safety right now. I wish we would pack our wagons and go to Philadelphia at once. *Later* we can seek justice for the Indians.

But Papa believes that we should not go anywhere until God tells us to go.

I fear I spoke crossly to him, asking how he will know when God wants us to go.

He looked at me sadly, as if mourning my lack of faith. "Dost thee know the words of our Quaker founder, Caty? 'In the light, wait, where unity is.'"

"I know the words," I whispered.

"If thee stands in the light, Caty, thee will always know the right thing to do," he said. "There is a still, small voice in each of us that speaks for God."

Have I heard this voice? I truly do not know which voice is God's, which is mine, or which is Papa's or Mother's inside me. Or, for that matter, Lucy's or Molly's or Master Collins's!

Papa saw my despair and bid me to go calm Mother. He believes that doing good will always help one's spirit.

Papa sounded so peaceful in the twilight. I wish *he* would be my inner voice and speak wisely to me forever. But he is always being called upon to care for others, to give his tender help and advice to friends and relatives.

I despair that I shall never find my own way to stand in the light, or find my own still, small voice.

28th of Eleventh Month, 1763

When Thomas and I went to school this morning, there was a great stir. Everyone was talking about the Indian raids. The attack appears to have been much worse than Doctor Griffith led us to believe. Five adults and three small children were murdered and two older children taken captive.

The Cantwell boys went into hideous detail about what Indians do to their captives. They called the Indians "savages" and told tales of their mutilating white people — cutting off noses and ears and hands, roasting them alive over fires, and beating them to death as they run a gauntlet.

Jess Owen did not notice me at all, as he was busy proclaiming that he would scalp ten savages if they tried to capture him.

I wanted to say what Papa had told me, explain why the Indians were angry, even remind the boys of William Penn and his great regard for the red man. But such a speech would have been too bold for me. Besides, it would not have been well received, for all were enjoying despising the enemy.

By day's end, Thomas and I were much frightened by all the talk. When we started our walk home, a screeching sound came from the forest. We whooped with fear and ran all the way back to the farm, shouting for Papa. When

Thomas imitated the sound, Papa assured us it was just a wild turkey.

30th of Eleventh Month, 1763

Today the Knowlton family came by in their wagon, on their way to the safety of Philadelphia.

Papa was away in the field. Mr. Knowlton said that when he comes home, he should pack us up and follow. The Delaware attacked another family last night, scalping all, even a two-year-old boy.

Mother raised her voice in anger. "I despise them! I despise them for bringing such terror down upon us!" she said.

Thomas, Eliza, and Baby Will all started to cry, and I took them inside and tried to divert them, until Papa came home.

After he comforted Mother, I followed him out to the woodpile where he had begun to cut logs.

"What is God saying to thee now?" I asked.

"The Almighty urges us not to fear rumors,

Caty. The Almighty even urges us not to place the bar on our door tonight."

I was so alarmed I was near tears. But Papa insists we must show confidence rather than fear. We must prove to the Indians that we trust them. We must not even draw the shutters!

So now our door is unlocked and our shutters are wide open, and everyone sleeps but me. I anxiously keep watch, "like a sparrow alone on the housetop."

Papa believes a plain act of trust will save us. But I believe he is trifling with our safety, and I am angry like Mother. Truly I am.

4th of Twelfth Month, 1763

Papa still does not lock the door. But Mother has exerted her will and not allowed Thomas and me to walk to school the last several days, for she fears we will be captured along the way. The path we take is over a mile long and much of it through lonely fields and forests, with no farm in sight.

So Thomas helped Papa stock the woodpile today while I fed the chickens. I try to have Papa's faith, but I confess I jumped whenever the tree branches rattled in the wind or shadows shifted.

5th of Twelfth Month, 1763

Today I helped Papa, Cousin Ezra, and Thomas bind the sheaves and pile the hay. I stopped often and stared at the fields. It being foggy, I thought once that I actually saw figures creeping through the corn rows.

I rushed to Papa and reported what I saw. He became cross when I pointed to the empty fog and asked me why I have so little faith.

Now in the dark, I hear every acorn and hickory nut that falls upon the roof, and I think, Are Indians surrounding us?

I hear a creak of the ladder steps, and my scalp tingles. Is one now climbing to the loft with a hatchet?

I am fearful this will be my last night on

Earth. But I am doubly fearful because my fear is not pleasing to God or Papa.

6th of Twelfth Month, 1763

I am still much frightened. But Papa seemed forgiving of my fear today and kindly told me to stay in the house and help Mother tend Baby Will.

Thomas has a toothache. Mother boiled corn-meal and milk, placed the gruel in a cloth, and pressed the hot poultice against his cheek.

Eliza is well now. We sat by the fire and I showed her how to string the dried pumpkin. Then we sat in the doorway, bathed by the golden light of the sunset, and I taught her to shuck corn. For a four-year-old, her fingers are unusually quick and nimble.

During daily devotions, Papa read Psalm 23 to bolster our courage, so that we will all fear no evil.

Still I prayed tonight he would put the bar on the door. But I think he has not.

7th of Twelfth Month, 1763

Everything was apples today. Mother, Eliza, and I made applesauce and apple butter and hung strings of apples to dry from the kitchen rafters.

Writing by the dim light of my candle, I still smell apples. The sweet scent rises from the dark downstairs and makes me feel unafraid — especially as I just heard Papa put the bar on the door. Hurrah!

8th of Twelfth Month, 1763

Cool and windy. Thomas and I piled corn high in the corncrib for the animals' winter food.

Silas Jones came to our farm. He shall accompany Papa and Cousin Ezra to the Meeting House tomorrow to discuss the problem concerning the Indians.

After dinner Mother and I carded wool before the fire. Thomas made a corn husk doll for

Eliza. Papa and Silas Jones talked about taking a trip to Philadelphia someday to see the Governor and discuss fair treatment for the Indians. They wish the English would make a formal land treaty with the Indians and, for once, honor all of its terms.

Before bed, Papa led us in prayer. He asked God to help us exert ourselves more to protect our red brothers, to wipe the tears from their eyes, and to comfort their afflicted hearts.

A bitter wind is leaking through the rafters. Soon the darkest day of the year will be upon us. I pray that the roaming Indian attackers have returned to their villages near the Susquehanna and now sit by their own fires with their own families.

Let there be no more fear and trembling, on either side.

10th of Twelfth Month, 1763

Fog on the fields early morning. But it was a sunny day. Mother and I baked all day and Thomas made candles.

Good news! Our prayers have been answered. Papa and Cousin Ezra and Silas Jones came back from the Meeting House this afternoon and announced that the valley is safe again.

A delegation of our Moravian neighbors has visited a council of the Delaware and reports that the Indians say they shall no longer attack white settlements, though they are still grieved over the recent encroachments on their land.

Mother was so relieved that she made a big dinner of ham, beans, squash, corncakes, and apple pie. And she said that Thomas and I could return to school tomorrow.

I pray the Indian scare has banished Jess Owen's memory of my stupid remark about his "impudent tongue." My face still reddens when I think of it. I must force myself to speak new words to him — to wipe away the stain of the old.

Today Jess Owen smiled at me as if my words had been completely forgotten. Then he boldly stated that he had missed me. And I answered, "I, thee."

I cannot believe I said that. "I, thee!" He must think I am the most daring girl in the country. He must think I am ready to marry him.

We studied how to divide the long numbers today and good news — I understand it! I have been afraid of this task for a very long time. I once peeked ahead at some problems in Master Collins's sum-book, and I nearly fainted — I saw trillions divided by billions!

But now the dreaded lesson has come and gone, and I am no longer afraid of dividing long numbers. This is one of God's tender mercies, I suppose.

But — *I, thee!* How I dislike *my* impudent tongue.

19th of Twelfth Month, 1763

Weather raw and cold. We begin Christmas baking tomorrow. Over forty people shall come to our farm after Monthly Meeting, including Jess Owen with his mother and father. He will see me in my own house, with my family — and I will be frozen with nerves and embarrassment. Thus I am dreading the Holy Day. My vanity causes me to neglect its divine meaning.

Worse still, I yearn for a blue ribbon to wear when he comes. Only I would not want him to think I was wearing it for him. Not ever.

24th of Twelfth Month, 1763

Industrious days. We peeled turnips and potatoes. We baked johnnycakes, sweet biscuits, six loaves of bread, pumpkin pudding and squash pudding, and eight pumpkin pies. We grated corn and stewed dried apples. Then we cleaned candlesticks, churned butter, scrubbed, and scoured. Blessedly, I have been too busy to worry about Jess Owen — and now I am too weary.

25th of Twelfth Month, 1763

At first the sun shone unseasonably warm. Then it grew cooler, and the sky turned gray. By mid-afternoon, after Meeting, it was quite cold, and puffy snow clouds gathered.

As the carriages arrived, I tended a pack of little ones in the big field. We played tag, then flew Thomas's kite.

I was racing across the grass, trying to make the kite soar, when I saw Jess Owen arrive with his kin. He had that "touch of a smirk" smile on his face. It was enough to make me lose all restraint and run like a wild horse — in the opposite direction. For joy and fear I ran through the cold air, urging the little ones on.

Though Eliza called for me to slow down, I could not rein in my high feelings. So I kept going till I ran into the forest, and the kite was caught by the trees.

Thomas called for Jess to untangle the string.

While Jess climbed a tall oak, I escaped and ran back to scoop up Baby Will and the little Collins girl. I took them to the swing near the barn where I started pushing them madly.

Finally the dinner bell rang. I carried the babies to the spring and washed all the little hands presented to me. Inside, at the table, forty Friends were gathered around three wooden tables, and I myself was seated across from Jess Owen!

I could not look at him face-to-face, so I stared with uncommon interest at my sweet potatoes, corn, and roasted turkey.

It may have seemed to him that I was lost *in* myself. But in truth, I was lost *to* myself. Completely. I could not find even the simplest thought to share.

I thought the night would never end. But gradually the guests gathered their things to leave. As Jess and his parents started to go, he came near me and wished me a blessed Christmas. "I hope the New Year fares well with thee," he said.

"I wish the same for thee," I said.

"The New Year will be fine — if thee is a part of it," he said.

"Thee is kind," I said.

Then he climbed into his carriage, and as they drove off, it started to snow. I think for once I said the right thing.

My candle burns in the dark while the wind gently swirls the snow against the window.

Thank you, dear Almighty, for this perfect night and for the birth of Thy son, Jesus Christ, our Lord.

27th of Twelfth Month, 1763

Rain mixed with snow. A sad, swampy day.

At candlelight, Reverend Beckwell from the Moravian fort knocked on our door. He told Papa that yesterday a mob party had presented itself to the Conestoga Indians at Lancaster and threatened to murder them on the spot if they did not leave. The mob was revenging the deaths of the settlers in Eleventh Month.

These Indians, however, were innocent of those crimes. In fact, they were all Christians.

Nevertheless, all of them, women and children included, were forced to quickly remove themselves from their camp. They even left behind their harvest.

30th of Twelfth Month, 1763

The Reverend wants Papa and other Quaker Friends to ride to Lancaster tomorrow and help protect the frightened Indians on their sad march to Philadelphia.

We passed the Sabbath in much silence and prayer. When Papa began to read, "The Lord preserveth all them that love Him," he stopped and could not read further. I think his heart especially aches for the little Indian children.

For the first time in weeks, I am anxious again that the Indians might attack us. I do not want to lose the victory I have so recently gained: the triumph over my terrors. I pray passionately for peace for all.

This rainy night is as dismal and black as my heart. Before Papa and others could go help the Indians at Lancaster, terrible news was reported to the Moravians. As the tribe prepared to flee to safety, a drunken party of white men returned and reviled them. Though the Indians begged for mercy, the mob murdered them, the small children included.

All day Papa was so sorrowful he could barely speak. His strong feelings afflicted us all. After a cold dinner, Mother made me take Eliza and Thomas up to the loft early, so she and Papa could be alone.

Eliza was tired and went to sleep quickly. But I heard Thomas sniffling, and I lit the candle.

I asked why he was crying, and he said he wept for the persecution of the Christian Indian babies, and he wished Papa was not unhappy and everyone would be safe.

I told him to close his eyes and find a calm place within himself. Then I stroked his damp, brown hair until he breathed peacefully in sleep.

Comforting Thomas has served to comfort me.

6th of First Month, 1764

At Meeting today, Papa broke the silence.

He told the Friends that the Indians have trusted the white men and we have forsaken them. He reminded them of William Penn and his great friendship with the Delaware. Papa recalled that a Delaware chief once said: Whenever Quakers are nearby, the Indians sleep in peace. The Indians have thought themselves happy in their friendship with us.

But now, the backwoodsmen are destroying the red men with liquor and smallpox and murder. There are many who believe the Indian has no more soul than a buffalo. Even many Quaker Friends think of them as "savages." (Indeed, I have even heard Mother call them such.) Drunken murderers have fired and burnt to the ground Indian village after Indian village. Why can the Governor not try harder to protect the innocent? It is *truth* we must strive for, Papa said, not *victory*.

Papa's voice shook, causing some Friends to stir. I believe he may have spoken with too much anger for their taste.

I pray that we will not be sent to school tomorrow. Could the slaughter of the Indians cause some to rise against us? Could bands of warriors be planning now to swoop down and avenge those who were murdered?

Perhaps at this moment, an Indian in the forest spies upon me and sees me write by candle. Perhaps he sees me mouth a prayer: "Examine me, O Lord, and prove me. Try my reins and my heart."

Sadly, I am more frightened than ever. I must blow out my light.

7th of First Month, 1764

Dear God, save us. We are captured.

8th of First Month, 1764

Dear Papa, I hope these words will find thee. My captors stare coldly as I write.

9th of First Month, 1764

Papa, one grabbed my diary from me and showed it to other three. They studied it, then returned it to me.

Now I tremble, but write quickly to explain. On the way to school four painted Indians came out of bushes. One caught me. Another caught Thomas and threw him across his shoulder.

Thomas fought. When he fell to the ground, I screamed at him to run. Two Indians chased after him, and all disappeared into woods.

Other two dragged me away.

Both Indians are painted red and black and have shaved heads. One seems quite old, but his grip is strong, and I cannot fight him.

Papa, I scribble a few words. Have lost track of days. I am so frightened I cannot think. I only obey them like a slave.

I write when I can, Papa. One day blends into the next. Now we are camped under a cliff. The old one tries to give me roasted meat. I choke and vomit. If they scalp or burn me alive, I pray God take my soul quickly. God save Thomas wherever he is.

Papa, Thomas is with me now. They brought him to our camp at dawn. I held him tight and told him to be strong. Holding him gives me strength. But strength for what? Our execution and torture? Where are we going? Help us, God.

I write whenever they sleep or are otherwise occupied. Only twice have they caught me — and then they seemed more curious than angry. They pointed to my book and spoke to one another, then let me alone.

Thomas is silent with shock, Papa. I gnaw my tongue in anguish. I fear they will kill him if he remains afflicted.

Papa, all day I gripped Thomas's hand and willed him to walk. He never spoke, except for whimpers.

What day is it now? I have lost all track of time.

We camped in a clearing. The old man made a shelter of boughs while others hunted. I do not know where we are. Or where they are taking us. Is it even the same day as when last I wrote?

Will they murder us in a savage ceremony? I am so horrified, I am numb, Papa.

The Indians caught a deer, skinned it, and roasted it over the fire. Still unable to eat or speak, Thomas fell into a fitful sleep. It was good he slept and did not see what happened next. Two Indians took bloody scalps from a bag. They dried them and scraped them by the fire. They must have scalped victims on their hunt.

I vomited.

At dawn, I could not get Thomas to stand. The Indians stared hard at him — except for the old man who seems not to hear or see us. I whispered urgently, "Thee must stand. Stand for Papa, Mother, Baby Will, Eliza. They want thee to stand." When he stood and walked, I felt a horrible guilt, for I cannot promise him that he will ever see thee again.

We traveled footpaths all day, then camped under a rock shelter. They tried to feed us corn-meal, but neither of us could eat. We are cold and weak now. I think we will die soon, Papa.

Thomas lived through the night, but is very feeble. At dawn, he looked at me with hollow eyes. With all the might of God, I willed him to walk in front of me over the narrow path. Over and over, I whispered, "Thee must walk for Papa."

The Indians watch Thomas like hawks. If he drops, I fear they will scalp him.

Thomas fell and lay lifeless. One Indian walked toward him with a hatchet. I screamed and threw myself over his body. I told them they must kill me first.

The old Indian looked at me with keen interest. He spoke to others, then crouched before Thomas and whispered to him.

Thomas opened his eyes and smiled. I think he was half-insane.

But the old Indian smiled back. He fed Thomas cornmeal from his pouch. Then he picked him up and put him over his shoulder and carried him.

The other three followed, and I came last, trembling and wiping tears.

Now all sleep. A wolf howls beyond our fire light. Lord, bear me up for the sake of Thomas.

Thomas still does not speak, Papa. Again, all day the old Indian carried him in his arms and shared his food with him. We waded an icy river, then climbed into a canoe, and hacked through thin ice to move downriver.

Where do we go? How many days have we been gone? How far are we from thee now? Papa, do not forget us.

Perhaps it has been a week since our capture, Papa. I cannot tell. Today we passed a burned settlement and saw charred bodies on the riverbank. I held Thomas against me so he could not see. The old Indian watches me with dark, unfathomable eyes. Will they burn us, too?

Second day on the river. At twilight the Indians camped on shore, peeled bark from trees and built a shelter held up by four logs. I tried to eat cornmeal and smoked fish, but cannot swallow.

In the afternoon, the sound of drums came from the forest beyond the shore. Smoke was rising into the gray sky.

As they took us ashore into Indian camp, dogs barked, and children ran to stare. Women and men stood frozen, watching us. Maybe fifty in all.

Our captors led us to a hut, and a frail-looking old woman took us inside. There was an open fire in the middle of the room. In the dim light, we sat on animal skins and drank water from a gourd.

A young woman sat with us. She had a handsome face and very long black hair. She tried to feed us gruel of cornmush, but we spat it up like babies. She and the old woman draped pungent skins over us and left.

Now we are alone. The hut is one room with a hole in the roof to let out smoke from the fire. Strips of corn, dried pumpkin, and clumps of roots and tobacco hang from the ceiling.

Thomas lies curled like a wounded animal.

I fear we face torture in the morning, Papa, like the burnt bodies on the river. I would try to escape, but Thomas is too weak to run with me. I will die before I forsake him.

At dawn the old Indian came to us. A young man was with him. He picked up Thomas and took him from me. We both screamed.

I tried to run after him, but the two women held me down. I fought desperately, for I could hear Thomas cry my name, the first words he has spoken in days. The sound was terrible to my ears, such that I fainted.

I felt hands stroking my face, and I opened my eyes. The thin, old woman was kneeling beside me, painting my face red. I begged her to bring Thomas back to me. The young woman — her daughter, I think — rubbed my arms with bear grease. I begged them both. But they do not understand me.

I tried to stand, but collapsed. Tears streamed down my face, mixing with red paint, like tears of blood.

They left me alone, but stand guard by the entrance while I suffer and anguish for Thomas.

The old woman and her daughter painted me again. They smeared bear grease into my hair and combed it smooth with a bristle brush. The daughter took off my torn shoes, tenderly washed my feet with water, then put soft moccasins on them. Her baby is nearby, tied to a straight, thin board. A fat, round-faced baby with black eyes.

Papa, I believe I have been adopted as the old woman's second daughter. Yesterday, after I was painted, the two women removed my torn cloak and dress and put me in a fringed shirt and a deerskin skirt.

I pleaded for news of Thomas, but they behaved as if they did not hear. I kept asking for him, red tears falling. Twice more they had to paint me.

The old woman brought me a corncake. I stared at it, desiring never to eat again, only to sink into death. But then I thought, God wills me to live, in order that I might save Thomas. So I did try to swallow their food.

Next they pulled me to my feet, draped a robe of feathers over my shoulders, then led me into the cold, windy sunlight. We walked to a longhouse covered with bark.

I hoped that Thomas would be inside the house, but he was not. Only many Indians crowded into a dark, smoky area.

They sat me before a group. All stared, a drum beating softly, to match the fearful beating of my heart.

Insanely I thought of Mother's rules for Meeting and recited them like catechism.

A man spoke in Indian. The old woman came forward and gave a long speech. Her thin body shook with emotion as her reedy voice cried out in anguish.

She handed the man a necklace of white shells. He turned to me and spoke loudly, saying, "Chilili," then handed me over to her.

She and her daughter tried to embrace me, as if I were now their kin. Though their touch was tender, I was as lifeless as a stone statue.

They sleep now while I write. The black-eyed baby stares curiously at me in the dim light.

Alone now, Papa. I have not yet seen Thomas. For three days I have sat in the old woman's cold, smoky hut, dressed like an Indian, stinking of bear grease.

Whenever the old woman and her daughter call me "Chilili" and speak to me, I pretend not to hear. I only stare at the fire, trying to cling to my past life. But my mind is invaded by odors from the grease in my hair and the beaver pelts draped over my shoulders. A strange and savage dream has overtaken my life.

The two women stare at me as I write. But they do not seem to mind. Instead they appear curious and respectful. Perhaps they think my writing is some sort of magic.

Today I hauled wood. Trudged back and forth with a tall young Indian who has an eagle painted on his cheek. He cut dead tree limbs with his hatchet, and I picked them up and helped him carry them back to the hut.

I never spoke. Only trudged in perpetual, sorrowful silence. How many days have passed?

The fat Indian baby coos and laughs as his mother plays peekaboo with him. He never appears fretful like Baby Will. Forgive me, Papa, but I wonder bitterly why God dost make this savage child more healthy and happy than His own Christian baby.

Sometimes in the hush of night, I think I hear Thomas cry my name. But it is only the devil torturing me, Papa.

Went into the frozen marsh to check traps with three hunters, including the one with the eagle painted on his cheek. They thrust a freshly-caught beaver carcass into my arms and I followed them, blood dripping onto the snow.

Scraped pelts with the old woman and her daughter while the daughter's baby sleeps on his board. They try to befriend me, say "Chilili," and smile, but I do not answer. Their tender treatment will not soften me. I will never be adopted by them.

The young woman holds her quiet, bright-eyed baby and stares at me in the dim firelight. No matter how cold I am toward her, she treats me with courtesy and calm. She wears buckskin decorated with shells and brightly colored porcupine quills. Her long, shiny hair is pulled back and tied with a piece of cloth. Her eyes are dark and warm. But I despise her, Papa. She let them take Thomas from me. I will not ever be kind to her. Forgive me, but I despise her red baby, too.

Thus far, none seem to care that I write. My spirit would fade completely if I could not write, Papa. I pray these words reach thee and Mother someday.

Helped hunters check traps again. We were silent, walking single file on the snowy, wet path. Then we all returned in the wind and heavy rain.

I slipped and fell. One tried to help me, but I pushed him away. I should die if any of them touch me. They are more animal to me than the bloody game I help carry. I pretend I am dead in their world.

Weary and faint-hearted. God give me strength until I find out for certain if Thomas is dead.

Hot with fever. Wet coldness has chilled me to bone — cannot get warm. Teeth chatter. Cough dreadfully — can no longer write.

Thomas is either dead or faraway and I will not see him again. I know this. But I do not care. I do not care for anything. Though I live, I feel dead.

Why am I here? Why did they take Thomas? Why did God let us be captured? I prayed so hard for us all to be safe, Papa, and God didn't hear.

Burned with fever all day. In and out of dreams, heard rattle shaking over me, and low, steady singing. Now I am alone. Cough worse.

Today the old woman and her daughter tortured me. They put me in a low bark house and poured water over hot stones. Steam blinded me as extreme sweat rolled off my skin.

Then they forced me to drink a terrible concoction, pulled me out of the sweat oven, dunked me down into a hole they had made in the river ice, into the freezing water, then wrapped me tightly in woolen cloths and lay me near the fire, turning me like meat on a stick till I was dry.

I cannot explain why I feel better now. Their torture has strangely healed me.

Fever and sweating have thawed my heart. Now I feel it might burst from sorrow. I think of thee all, Papa — of Mother singing to Baby Will as she rocks him, of Eliza's little fingers shucking corn. And of Thomas — Papa, I can hardly write of Thomas. He was a good, brave little boy. Why did God punish him so cruelly? I feel unceasing anguish and cannot stop my tears.

I hear flute music coming through the cold dark, and my memory flutters wildly. Papa, I see thee at dusk, near the woodpile. I see Mother sewing and Eliza laughing. I run with Thomas toward the schoolhouse as the bell clangs.

I am sighing for every detail of my old life, even arithmetic and the ache of sitting still in

Meeting. All seems so sweet mingled with the flute music, while I am in exile from everything I know and love. It was better when I was frozen, Papa, when I felt nothing. I yearn to find my way back to thee. But I cannot make a plan of escape till I have knowledge of Thomas.

Storm rages outside. Wind howls. Many sit in our hut, telling stories and eating smoked fish. The baby waves his arms and cries out happily, making the women laugh. The hunter with the eagle painted on his cheek watches me as I write.

There. I just looked at him sternly, and he looked away.

At least they allow me to write. Indeed I believe they think my writing is something extraordinary. Each time I take out my copybook and quill, I see looks of approval pass from one to another.

Perhaps if they knew how bitterly I wrote about them, they would not be so pleased.

Now I must conserve my words, for my ink is low.

Last night I dreamt that I went for water. When breaking the ice, I saw a small boy floating in the air up the hill beyond the river, and I thought, Thomas? My God, is it Thomas?

I started shouting to him. But he disappeared over the hill, and I woke up, trembling. In the dark, the Indian baby whimpered. He so rarely cries, that for a moment, I felt a tenderness for him and longed to comfort him.

Dear God, bring Thomas back to me, and take us home to Baby Will. Dear God, give me courage. Make me strong. Help me to live.

Something strange happened to me today, Papa. Without warning, I began to say all my thoughts out loud. And many of them were most bitter. It happened when I was walking behind the hunter with the eagle painted on his cheek. I slipped and fell in the snow. After I scrambled back to my feet, my wrath poured out like fire. I told him that I was not a savage like him and the others! I told him that I despised them. I despise everything about him and his people. They are all heathens, with no God. They are all animals and are all going to the devil!

As strange as my behavior was, his behavior was stranger. He did not turn back even once to look at me, nor to command me to be silent. Indeed, I began to wonder if he had heard me at all.

Then, I wondered if I had even spoken. Was I only thinking these venomous thoughts?

I shouted in an angry voice, demanding to know if he had heard me speak.

But still he did not look back at me.

I fear I am going mad, Papa. Perhaps invisible, too. Worst of all, my ink is nearly gone.

What will I do, Papa? This is the last of my ink. Now for certain, I will totally disappear.

I can write again. I was so desperate for ink that I begged the whole camp to help me. But all looked at my empty jar with dumb bewilderment. In despair, I hurled it across the snow.

But when I rose at dawn, I found the jar at the entrance to our hut. It had been replenished with ink made from coal dust. And a new wild turkey quill was with it!

I lost all restraint again and I shouted at the camp, asking who had given me these writing tools. I held the jar and quill up to the old woman and her daughter and demanded to know. But the old woman only pressed her finger to her cheek.

Perhaps an angel delivered these gifts to me in the night, and I can call them a miracle.

Papa, why am I suddenly turned out of myself — shouting and exclaiming? Is it because I do not care any more what others think? This is a new and frightening thing.

I pray for the ability to hide again. But some great urge seems to be pushing me out of myself.

I talked behind the hunter's back again today. On the path, as we were returning from a fox hunt, I told him about the miracle of my ink. I spoke loudly and clearly and explained that my God had sent ink to me. I told him how the Lord had once turned water into wine and fed five thousand with only two fishes and five loaves of bread.

I asked him what he thought of all that. And when he did not respond, I could not keep quiet my opinion that he was as dumb as an ox!

I know I am going a little mad, Papa. But 'tis curious that yelling in this manner has begun to make me cheerful.

I keep talking, Papa!

Now when the old woman and her daughter call me "Chilili" and speak to me in Indian, I answer them in English and say whatever I like.

Today, when they spoke to me, I told them plainly and honestly that I do not care what they have to say, I have great grief in my heart and I have great anger. I told them I miss my family and demanded to know where Thomas is. I shouted that they must bring him back to me! "Only then — when that happens — will I be nice to thee!" I told them.

They watched patiently, then went about their work, praying, I imagine, that this wild spirit will leave me soon.

I declare it will not. I have found strange pleasure in my new freedom to speak my mind.

Tonight I attended a campfire ceremony. I stood alone watching young men and women move their feet to the pulse of the rattle and the eerie singing of the older women.

I would not join them. When the leader of the dance spoke to me in Indian, I was impudent, telling him that I had no desire to dance like a heathen. "Kill me if thee likes!" I said. "Burn me! Torture me! My spirit will go to God and I will find comfort and rest!"

He spoke calmly in Indian again, as if we were having a civil conversation.

Nearby the hunter with the eagle painted on his cheek danced. When I heard him laugh at me, I turned on him and spoke furiously, daring him to laugh again. I told him my words would make him wither if he understood them. Then I stalked away.

I can talk all I want. I can say anything I like, and no one tries to stop me. Today when small children gathered around, I berated them, saying, "Thee are nothing compared to Thomas, Eliza, and Baby Will! My brothers and sister are the most precious beings on Earth!"

They stared dumbly.

"Thee are all so dreadfully stupid!" I shouted.

Though they do not understand my tongue, they understood my rage, and when one tiny girl began to cry, I felt stricken.

I returned to my hut and wept.

Papa, thee always said the best help is in thyself. But if thyself is filled with darkness and inward suffering, where is the light then to sustain thee? I am made of so little strength and goodness that I cannot find help within.

Today I went again with the hunters to carry their game. Once more, I found myself on the narrow path, walking behind the hunter with the eagle painted on his cheek, and once more some mysterious force pried the secrets from my heart. I confessed to him that I felt peculiar hearing myself talk so much, for in my world, I had recently been afraid to talk at all.

I told him that at home, I have feared sounding too bold or too vain. But perhaps I am both these things, I explained. Bold and vain may be my true qualities, and I don't know what to do about them. I fear I may someday be turned out from the Society of Friends. I may be an outcast and never find a husband or have a family.

I confessed all this to him and further grieved that my fears are ridiculous because most likely I will never see my home again, ever. I wept pitifully as hot tears fell upon the dead fox I carried.

The hunter never turned around.

Had I spoken at all?

I have no idea what month or day it is. But it must be late winter, for the sap has begun to run. Today I trailed after the old woman's daughter through the woods. Men drew the sap from trees into bark receptacles. Women boiled it by dropping in hot stones, then we poured some on the snow to eat.

Back at the hut, the old woman melted bear's fat with the maple sugar and we dipped roasted venison into it, and our cornbread, too.

A good meal, not unlike a special supper cooked by Mother. I tried to scorn it, but I ate all I was given and wanted more.

Papa, how can I die of grief when I have so large an appetite? Why does life cling to a cruel world with such ferocity?

I dreamt again of Thomas last night. He was on the other side of the hill, beyond the frozen river. He was being tortured — beaten to death with sticks as he ran a gauntlet. I woke up in anguish.

All day I have wanted to slip away and look on the other side of the hill. But I will have to cross the frozen river first, and I do not know how solid the ice is. Perhaps I will test it when I fetch water in the morning.

Am I going mad, Papa, chasing after a dream?

At dawn, I went to the river for water. Rather than break the ice, I attempted to walk on it. I stepped carefully, until I heard a crack. Then I jumped back, just in time.

When I turned around, I saw the hunter standing nearby.

I shouted at him angrily, asking him why he spied on me. I told him that I had seen my brother in a dream, that the Indians were beating him to death.

He shook his head.

"Why dost thee say no?" I asked with wonder. "No what? Dost thee understand me?"

He looked long and hard into my eyes, then turned and left.

"Thomas is being tortured!" I screamed.

Then I thought I heard him speak — in *English* words. I thought I heard him say, "No. He is not."

But his back was to me, and the wind was blowing. So perhaps I did not hear a thing.

Now I sit alone, in the dark, listening to the wind. It seems to mock me. "No. He is not" — can the wind sound like it is speaking English words?

Not truly.

But it *must* have been the wind.

Another dream of Thomas on the other side of the hill. He was chasing our pig Curly with a stick. I yelled at him to stop . . . then Curly changed into a monstrous bear and turned on us both.

Why do I keep dreaming about the hill? I am desperate now to climb it.

But first I must cross the river.

Later, when all are asleep, I will go in the dark and find a path where the ice is solid.

The moon is almost round tonight.

Last night my plan was crossed by a sudden storm. Snow whirled, and clouds covered the moon. I could not see at all, thus did not venture onto the ice.

Today dawns bright with the sun shining on the snow like a million pieces of broken glass. Perhaps the river ice has become more solid, and tonight it will support my footfall.

Papa, it has grown dark. But the moon is bright outside. It is the perfect night for my journey over the hill to search for Thomas.

If I am drowned in the icy river, or slain by my captors, forgive my vanities. I have been half out of my mind and consumed by anguish.

The old woman, her daughter, and baby grandson sleep now. I must hurry into the starry moonlight. Remember, I love thee and Mother with all my heart. Caty.

The Bible says after the winds and earthquake and fire, there was a still, small voice. I heard it last night, Papa. Only it was not God's. Or mine.

In the moonlight, I found the river covered with new snow. Seized with the desire to find out if Thomas were on the other side of the hill, I started across the ice.

Soon it began to crack. But locked in the grip of my will, I could not turn back. I kept going.

Then came a giant crack. Both my legs crashed through the ice, and I plunged down into the icy water.

I grabbed a broken shard. Clinging desperately, I heard "Chilili!"

In the moonlight, I saw an Indian standing on the riverbank, holding out a branch. *In English*, he commanded, "Take it!"

I grabbed the branch. The rough bark cut my hands as I gripped tightly and pulled myself onto stronger ice. Then I leapt to the bank and fell onto the snow.

When the Indian helped me up, I saw he was the hunter with the eagle painted on his cheek.

I shook all over — whether from relief of being saved, or simply from the cold, I know not. Through chattering teeth I asked, "How dost thee know English?"

"I was English once," he said in a whispery, halting voice. "Now Lenape."

Then he turned and walked away, and I was left still trembling.

My hand is steady now as I write close to the fire while the others sleep. A thought strikes me.

Many days ago, when I asked who had replenished my ink, the old woman touched her cheek. Was she referring to the hunter with the eagle painted on his cheek? Did she mean that *he* had refilled my jar?

I watch the fire smoke waft up through the hole in the ceiling into the silent night sky. I am filled with confusion, Papa, and wonder.

I did not see the hunter all day. I would think I had dreamt our meeting if it were not for the raw, red spots on my hands from clinging to the branch he held out to me.

I am anxious to see him again. Surely he can help me gain news of Thomas.

Where is the hunter?

All this rainy day I worked with the women as we made moccasins in the longhouse, and I did not lay eyes upon him. I looked around the camp whenever I had the excuse to fetch water or wood. But he is nowhere to be seen.

I cringe to think that the hunter understood all the wrathful words I spoke these past weeks, and I marvel he did not scorn me. Rather, he saved me from icy death. I feel chastened and humbled.

High winds today. River water rushing from the spring rains. Again I did not see the hunter. The more time passes, the more distressed I become.

The hunter is back!

Late this afternoon, he and two others returned with the carcass of a huge black bear. I hurried to the bear dance in front of the longhouse, desperate to speak with him.

The hunter danced hard to the drumbeat — shouting and leaping and stamping. He seemed so Indian in the firelight, I could not believe that he was once English.

He never looked my way. Not once.

Perhaps he plans not to speak my language again. Perhaps he will deny that he ever spoke to me at all.

Now that a door has been slightly opened and light has streamed in, I will die if it is slammed shut, and I am left in complete darkness again.

Today I worked with the old woman and her daughter, cutting out fat parts of the bear. We boiled them down until the grease rose to the surface. Then we skimmed the fat with a wooden spoon and put it into a skin bag. Several times they tried to engage me, but I refused to look them in the eye. I cannot be close to them, not until I know Thomas's fate.

I finally escaped our task and hurried into the woods to look for the hunter, but to no avail.

With a heavy heart, I returned to our hut. The old woman stared at me with a faint smile and said something to her daughter, pointing to her cheek. Then together, they laughed. How did she know that the hunter is the source of my distraction?

If she thinks my feelings for him are affection, she is horribly wrong. In truth, I am growing to despise him for playing tricks on me.

Early morning. I dreamt of Thomas again last night. Though he was very tiny, as small as Baby Will, he spoke in clear sentences: *Caty, I miss thee.*

Then a giant eagle came over the sky and the shadow of its wings hid Thomas and I could see him no more. I woke up, weeping. I will find the hunter today or burst from my anguish.

This afternoon I found the hunter in the woods with boys, stripping sheets of bark off the trees. I watched him as I collected kindling.

When he started back to the camp alone, I rushed forward. I did not exert patience but demanded that he talk to me. "Thee must stop torturing me!" I said.

He stared back with an impenetrable gaze, then started walking again.

I grabbed his arm and said, "Please, I humbly crave thy help to find Thomas. Thomas came to me in a dream and was covered by the shadow of an eagle!"

He made no response but broke free of my grasp and went on his way.

Now I sit in our hut at dusk. The old woman gives roots and herbs to a visitor outside. Her daughter pounds corn. The baby coos. But I feel separated from all that is human and loving. Alone in an ocean of darkness.

Dear God, I am grateful for the wonder of Thy ways. It has taken a heathen to remind me of the Psalms: "Protect us, O Lord, under the shadow of Thy wing."

A short time ago, as I lay awake with a bitter heart, I heard a clicking sound, as if someone were signaling outside.

I wrapped a fur robe around me and crept to the door. A figure stood in the cold dark. He whispered, "Chilili." It was the hunter.

I slipped outside to join him.

He spoke with great solemnity, saying, "Do not fear the eagle in your dream. It can be your brother's guardian."

"Is Thomas alive?" I asked him.

"Yes."

I burst into tears and wanted to throw my arms around him. But I restrained myself, and instead asked through my tears if he were the one who had replenished my ink. He smiled, then slipped away as quietly as he had come.

Now I terribly regret that I asked a trifling question about my ink and wasted a precious chance to find out about more important things! Where is Thomas? Is he well? When will I see him again? Why were we captured? When will we return home?

It must be spring now, Papa. I saw a ladybug on a dead leaf and caught sight of a baby deer when I was searching the woods for the hunter.

I finally found him and other men peeling bark from trees again to restore their huts. As I gathered nuts, I waited for a chance to talk with him.

When he was working alone, I moved closer to him. "Tell me, please," I begged. "Where is my brother?"

Without stopping his work or even gazing at me he said, "He lives with Black Snake, in another camp."

"Will thee take me to see him? Please?" I said.

He remained silent.

"Can thee tell me," I asked him, "why we were taken? When will we be returned to our family?"

In halting, crude English, he said we were captured because of the massacre of the Indians in Lancaster. We were given to the old woman and to Black Snake because both had lost children to measles.

Then, Papa, he gave me the worst news: We will be kept forever. "This is what the Great Spirit wants," he said.

"How dost thee know what the Great Spirit wants?" I begged.

He did not answer at once, and before I could rail against the Great Spirit, a young boy shouted for the hunter, and he started over to him.

"Just tell me one thing!" I cried out. "How is Thomas? Is he well?"

He turned and said simply, "He is growing in Indian ways."

I'm certain it is near the end of Third Month now. I saw rabbits today, and fresh anthills in the dirt. I hear tree frogs and spied a pair of geese on the river.

Today when I took my bucket to the water, I watched the hunter in the distance. He was fishing, as sudden warm weather has melted much of the ice.

Before he spied me, I tried to imagine him in britches and a white shirt, in riding boots, with a hat, but I could not. He seems completely Indian in all his ways.

He pulled up his line and began walking away.

I ran after him. "Wait," I called. "Please tell me, when was thee English?"

He shook his head as if I should not pry.

"Dost thee not miss thy people?" I asked.

He stared at me coldly. "The Lenape are my people," he said.

I fear I could not hold my tongue. I asked how he could turn against his fellow creatures and give himself over to being a savage.

I was not prepared for the torrent of angry words that spilled from him. "I scorn you because you do not think of the Lenape as fellow creatures," he said in a low, angry voice. "You do not know the names of the women who care for you. You do not try to learn our ways because you say we are animals. Like all the Christians, you lie. You preach love while all the time you think you are better than all people."

I was stunned by his wrath, but before I could defend myself, he walked away.

I shouted at his back, "I cannot lovingly regard thy people until I see my brother again!"

I wanted to say more, but he was too faraway to hear me.

The hunter's angry words have stolen my wrath. I am not so inclined now to batter the Indians with my insults.

Papa, I remember words thee often said during family worship, words uttered by one of the first Quaker Friends: "Our life is love and peace and tenderness; and being one with another, and forgiving one another, praying one for another, and helping one another up with a tender hand."

A thought has come to me: Though he did not admit to it, I am certain it was the hunter who replenished my ink — forgiving me when I was daily cursing him.

And did he not help me up with a tender hand when I nearly drowned?

I fear I cannot rise to the level of his kindness, Papa, nor to thine. My fear and concern for Thomas have killed the goodness in me. I fear the love in my heart is too measured and miserly.

So, if I am not a good Quaker, Papa, what am I?

I approached the hunter today with true humility. I used a friendly Indian greeting. I put my hand up and said, *"Hah."* From the old woman and her daughter, I have learned that this greeting seems to mean something akin to "Good be with you."

I smiled at him, perhaps my first smile since I was captured. And my heart grew lighter as he smiled back.

"Will thee take me to see Thomas?" I asked as humbly as I could.

He just stared at me.

"Soon?" I asked hopefully.

"When Black Snake says to come," he said and went on his way.

It must be Fourth Month now. Bees have returned, and tufted titmice sing in the woods. Trout lilies are in bloom. Today the old woman gathered fresh bloodroot and cowslip. All I can think is: Who is Black Snake? Where does he live? Is he kind to Thomas?

Today I humbly approached the hunter again. I could see him eye me warily, as if expecting me to beg once more to be taken to Thomas.

I surprised him: "What is the name of the old woman?" I asked.

His dark eyes brightened. His answer sounded like "Wapa-go-kos."

I have heard people say that name. "What does it mean?" I asked.

"White Owl."

I smiled. My regard for the old woman grew slightly, for a white owl is a beautiful creature.

He went on to tell me that the old woman's daughter's name is Tan-ka-wun, which means "Little Cloud." I like that name, too. The poetry of it somewhat warms my feelings for the long-haired girl.

It seems that her baby has no official name yet, but they call him Little One, which sounds like "Penk-won-wi."

When I asked the hunter for the meaning of his name, he told me his Lenape name, Wine-lo-wich, means "Snow Hunter."

A lovely name, I thought.

But, Papa, thee will be surprised to learn that mine is even more lovely. Chilili means "Snow Bird" in Lenape. He told me that it was the name of White Owl's younger daughter who died of measles, a disease brought to the forest by the white traders. I am White Owl's new younger daughter, he explained. And Little Cloud's new sister.

A wave of sorrow passed through me. Both for myself and for White Owl and Little Cloud. I can *never* be their daughter or new sister.

"Perhaps thee can call me by my Indian name," I told Snow Hunter. "But say it in English. And I will call thee Snow Hunter."

He agreed on this plan.

As he walked away from me, I called after him. "Snow Hunter! Will thee take me to see my brother soon? I miss him, like Little Cloud misses her sister."

At first I thought he was ignoring me. But then he looked back and gave me a quick nod and went on his way.

Praise God!

A warm and lovely day. For certain now it is Fourth Month. Mayapples are back, but not yet blooming.

In the twilight, White Owl returned from collecting plants, then very carefully shook the dirt from them.

She is a mystery, coming and going into the spring forest at odd hours, bringing back plants and bark, then boiling them down.

Everyone in the camp treats her with respect, and often someone asks for one of her potions.

As I watched her, she caught my eye, and I smiled, partly because I felt sorry for the loss of her younger daughter, Chilili.

White Owl nodded and smiled back. Then she returned to her plants, sparing me from too much attention.

Now that I know the meaning of her name, she seems more real to me, and less a "savage" stranger.

Tonight while White Owl and Little Cloud were baking corncakes, they talked softly and laughed together. As I listened to them, their gentle speech and laughter reminded me of Mother and me making supper together at home. I felt such sorrow I had to walk away.

The long-awaited happened today.

This morning, the sunlit river flowed rapidly, completely free of ice. As I drew water, Snow Hunter came upon me, silent as a deer. He asked if I wanted to see where my brother lived.

I nodded with wonder, afraid even to speak, for fear he might withdraw such a gift.

"Come," he said. And he headed down a trail that led along the river. I quickly followed, and soon we came to a narrow bend with large rocks, a place where we could easily cross.

When we got to the other side, we climbed the hill, the very hill I have seen in my dream! At the top, he pointed to a distant gathering of huts. Smoke rose from their chimney holes into the blue sky.

"Your brother lives there with Black Snake," Snow Hunter told me.

Tears came to my eyes and I started to run, but he quickly caught me and held me gently.

"We cannot go now. Later Black Snake will invite us, after your brother learns Indian ways." He spoke with such kindness, I could not feel anger, but only impatience.

I let out a sigh and stared at the distant camp.

"'Tis amazing," I said. "My dreams told me that Thomas lived on that side of the hill."

"The Great Spirit sent the dreams to you," Snow Hunter said simply.

He explained to me that the Great Spirit is king of all things on Earth. It is the sunrise, the sunset, the darkness, the rain and wind and snow. It creates all human beings by its thoughts.

I told him that one could say the Quakers are of a similar mind, for Quakers believe that all things have a bit of God in them.

He nodded.

Then in the gray twilight, he said it was time to go home, and we left. 'Twas strange, but I nearly took his hand as we walked down the hill together. I am beginning to feel a great trust in him.

When we reached the other side of the river, it was almost night. Before I knew it, he had quietly disappeared . . . into the darkness of the Great Spirit. And I made my way back to my hut alone.

We must be midway into Fourth Month, or well into spring. It rained all last night. But at dawn, the sky was rose-colored; the air was clean and cool.

When I went for water, I felt so exuberant that I slipped over the river rocks and climbed the hill.

A great flock of geese sailed through the sky, returning home from the south. Mist hovered over the sunlit fields.

I could barely see the camp. But I heard children shouting. Was Thomas among them? Was he running through the mist?

I longed to run down into the valley and race through the wet fields, arms outstretched, screaming, *Thomas, Thomas!*

But I kept my feelings still. If I anger Black Snake, it might mean harm to Thomas.

White Owl and Little Cloud often laugh with one another. They laugh at themselves, at their cooking, and at Little One. Did Chilili, their true daughter and sister, laugh with them? Sometimes I feel as if I am her ghost, watching them from afar, unable to break into their circle. I simply cannot understand their words or their ways.

Thinking these things, I feel sad, and do not know if it is for Chilili or myself.

Today the men and boys burned a number of trees, then cut them down. After they cleared the brush, the women raked the dirt into small mounds. This section of the village will be our garden.

The smell of the woodsmoke brought a new wave of homesickness over me, so I left the others and wandered down to the river. As I sat on a rock, Snow Hunter found me.

He told me he was sorry that the Great Spirit had caused his people to tear me from my family.

"It is not fair to blame everything on the Great Spirit," I told him. "It does not allow one to argue. It's like when Papa says that God does not want us to go to Philadelphia."

I imagine he did not understand me, but he sat quietly with me and seemed melancholy.

Papa, the truth is that I no longer despise Snow Hunter, White Owl, or the rest of their people. Our capture no longer seems their fault. It seems the result, rather, of great forces beyond all our power . . . a war between our Gods, not our small human selves.

I dreamt again of Thomas. He was not running with Indian children in the fields. He was deathly ill, lying on animal skins, in the delirium of a fever.

When I woke, I ran to Snow Hunter's hut. I called to him, and when he came out, I told him my dream.

He listened with great seriousness, then said decisively, "We will go to see Black Snake."

I hurried after him, joyful, yet apprehensive that we were about to risk Black Snake's anger.

We headed for the river, crossed the rocks, and climbed the hill. When we reached the top, the sun was so bright it blinded us.

As we started down the slope toward Black Snake's camp. I trembled with anticipation. Children ran to greet us. Men and women came forward to stare. They talked and pointed at me. Snow Hunter spoke to a woman, and she led us to a hut.

When we stepped into the dimly lit room, I saw Black Snake, the old Indian who had taken Thomas from me. He stood with a man who wore a wolfskin headdress and shook a rattle over a small body lying on a bearskin.

It was Thomas.

Before anyone could stop me, I rushed forward with a cry and knelt beside him. His eyes were closed, and his skin so pale it seemed he had already left this world.

But his tender face made my heart break open, and I wept and stroked his damp, hot cheek.

Many Indians gathered around and watched silently as I whispered to him. I said prayers and stroked his thin arms, until finally God opened Thomas's lovely eyes.

He stared at me with a dazed expression, and I told him that I was with him, and that he need not be afraid.

Light came into his eyes then, and he smiled.

I was allowed to stay with Thomas all day and night. I lay beside him and never stopped touching him or speaking gently to him. I reminded him about our past lives ... Papa, Mother, Eliza, Baby Will ... even Curly the pig, our chickens, and the rules Mother enforces in Meetings. I talked about how I had been afraid to divide the long numbers and how it was really nothing to be afraid of. I even tried to explain how it works. Then over and over, I told him I would not leave him, never, not ever; I would always be with him.

At sunrise, he sat up and asked for food.

Snow Hunter spoke a long time with Black Snake and the man in the wolfskin. Then he came to me and said he had told them about my dreams, and they agreed that the Great Spirit wanted Thomas to be with me.

Papa, in that moment, I could see it was *truth* they strived for, not *victory*.

Blinded by my tears, I thanked Black Snake. Then we wrapped Thomas in a deerskin cape. Snow Hunter picked him up and carried him out of the camp, over the rise, across the river rocks, and all the way home to White Owl's hut.

Thomas was pale and quiet when Snow Hunter finally laid him down. But White Owl gave him one of her medicines, and he opened his eyes.

Now I must lie down, too, while she sits with him, chanting softly. I am so weary, I almost imagine that her tender voice belongs to Mother. I am grateful to Black Snake. I forgive him everything.

White Owl and Little Cloud gave Thomas a sweat bath today. The same they gave me long ago — when I thought they were torturing me.

This time, I did not fear them, but helped them instead. We put Thomas in the bark structure and steamed him until great amounts of sweat poured from his small body.

They made him drink a tonic. Then we lowered him into the cold river water, swaddled him in cloth, lay him close to the fire, and gave him sassafras tea.

This treatment has been good for him. He sits up now in the hut and, with big eyes, stares at all of us. I watch him with a grateful, humble heart.

Thomas is even better today. Color glows in his cheeks — and best of all, Papa — that mischievous look in his eyes has returned!

White Owl's medicine continues to work wonders on Thomas. Today, like a little duck he followed me when I washed our bowls near the river and when I carried wood and water. He even tried to help me pound the corn into flour. As we worked, he said, "Caty, is thee mad at me?"

"Why would I be mad at thee, Thomas?" I asked.

"Because thee told me to run. And I did not run fast enough."

Looking away from him, I blinked hard to hide my tears. "No, Thomas," I said, "thee did *exactly* as God wanted thee to do."

Papa, thy boy continues to improve. He has a ravenous appetite. He still follows me everywhere, but he seems more like his old self. He even speaks Lenape words to White Owl! This morning, she smiled and shook her head after he spoke to her.

"What did thee ask her?" I asked him.

"If she had a horse for me to ride."

"A horse! Dost thee ride horses now?" I said.

It seems that Black Snake's oldest sons have taught Thomas to ride. And when I asked him if he did well, he told me he was the best rider in their camp!

Dost that not sound like our Thomas, Papa?

White Owl, Little Cloud, and I planted corn in the mounds of the garden. At nightfall, Snow Hunter stopped by our hut and spoke privately to Thomas.

Soon Thomas came running to me and, with shining eyes, told me that Snow Hunter wants him to camp with another boy in the guardhouse next to the garden. "To scare away the deer during the night!" he said.

Forgive me, Papa, if Thomas is turning into a small warrior. But it is so pleasing to have him well, I cannot refuse him. Or Snow Hunter, for that matter.

Thomas and I took care of Little One this afternoon when his mother and White Owl went to gather herbs. The baby's diapers are made of rabbit skin and lined with fresh cattail fluff. When we changed them, we washed the rabbit skin in the river, and replaced the soiled cattails with fresh ones.

White Owl has made a small hole in one of Little One's moccasins. The hole is meant to keep spirits from taking him away.

When I explained the hole to Thomas, I added that I wished we could do the same for Baby Will.

"For whom?" Thomas said.

Fear struck me. "Baby Will! Thy brother! Dost thee not remember?" I nearly shouted.

He did not answer. He simply said, "Oh," and

looked away. I could not tell if he had no interest in the matter or if he suffers too much confusion to talk about it.

Today Snow Hunter came to see Thomas again. His affection for Thomas made me wonder if Thomas does not remind him of himself long ago. "Was thee the age of Thomas when thee began to live with the Lenape?" I asked him.

He gave the briefest nod, but enough to prompt me to inquire further.

"What was thy name?" I asked.

"John," he answered simply.

"Where was thy farm?" I asked.

"I do not remember," he said, and from the stern way he spoke, I knew he had just ended the conversation.

Ten years from now, will Thomas also say, "I do not remember?"

Today Snow Hunter brought Thomas a whistle made from bird bone. When Thomas received the gift, he said, *"Wanishi."* He told me that Black Snake had taught him to say this — it means he is thankful.

Thomas tells me that *wishi* means "good" and *wulelemil* means "wonderful." He has learned a number of Lenape words.

Snow Hunter invited Thomas to help him and the other boys and men plant their tobacco today.

Thomas, for his part, looks upon Snow Hunter with awe and admiration. Perhaps that is because Snow Hunter carried him in his arms all the way here.

After they left for their work, I helped White Owl repair our moccasins.

Today Snow Hunter gave Thomas a hunting lesson. White Owl, Little Cloud, and I stood by and watched as he put on a deerskin cape that had the head of the deer attached. Wearing this "garment," Snow Hunter showed Thomas how to approach the deer — toe first, head down.

Then he put the cape on Thomas. But it was so huge, it completely hid Thomas's small body. To watch Thomas move on his tiptoes in a jerky fashion was so amusing that White Owl, Little Cloud, and I collapsed in laughter.

Am I standing inside their circle now, Papa? Am I growing a little more like Chilili every day?

Early morning.

I watch White Owl in the sunlight outside the entrance to our hut. Her bony arms move vigorously as she pulls bark from redbud branches and ties it into bundles. Over time she will give all the bundles to different women who come to our hut.

In the yellow haze of the early light, she reminds me a bit of Mother. She works from early morning until late at night, always stretching out her hand to help others.

Now that I have begun to see White Owl as a real person, not unlike Mother, equal to me or thee, a pure truth has opened up in me, Papa: If White Owl is truly an equal person, then how can white people bear the weight of our sin — the sin of our attacks against the Indians and the stealing of their land?

A warm day. Early morning Thomas and I went with White Owl and Little Cloud into the woods and helped them gather wild plants and bark.

We did not take the first plant we saw. Instead White Owl placed tobacco beside it and spoke words as if she were praying.

Later Snow Hunter explained that White Owl was praying to the spirit of the plant, thanking it for its help. And whenever she peels bark from a tree, she first prays to the spirit of the tree.

Snow Hunter calls these spirits *manetu*. They are in all of nature.

Today again Thomas and I went with White Owl and Little Cloud and watched them dig up a number of plants. Then we helped them peel bark from walnut trees.

On the way back, I tripped and fell, twisting my ankle.

Little Cloud helped me up, and, as I had trouble walking, she bid me to lean against her and we stumbled together, laughing.

Our laughter increased our strength and was as much a medicine as the wild roots we had gathered.

Tonight White Owl applied black walnut sap to my inflamed ankle. Then Thomas and I listened to White Owl tell a story, and though I did not understand what she said, I was comforted by the steady, soothing rhythm of her speech.

It must be the middle of Fifth Month now, Papa, for the dogwood are in bloom.

Snow Hunter, Thomas, and I saw three owls in the twilight. Owl is *kookhoos* in Lenape. The number one is *kwut-tee*, two is *neesh-shah*, three is *nah-xah*.

Oh, and rabbit is *moushkiingwaus*. We saw *neesh-shah moushkiingwaus* in the twilight, too.

Papa, sometimes I fear that if we learn Indian ways, it will take us deeper into our new world and further away from thee and Mother. Every day, I try to tell Thomas about our old life. But he seems to fear my words. He moves away from me and restlessly begins some other activity. I am afraid to force him to listen, Papa. I wish I knew what thee would want me to do.

Today the women planted beans next to the corn, so the bean vines will cling to the cornstalks. We planted squash between the mounds of corn plants, so that its huge leaves will shade the ground and keep down the weeds. Now all "the three sisters," as the Lenape call them, have been planted — corn, beans, and squash.

Until new food is harvested, we will keep eating dried meat and fish and nuts, stored in a pit lined with rocks and covered with bark.

For dinner, White Owl and Little Cloud boil the dried meat in water until it swells and becomes soft enough to eat.

Often we have the meat with corncakes. Thomas and I help crush the dried corn. It seems that all day long someone is pounding corn. We sift it through a *pawenikan*, a flat basket sieve. Then we mix the flour with hot water, mold it into cakes, and bake the cakes in hot ashes.

It tastes good, though I long for Mother's apple pie and pumpkin pudding.

Hot day, rainy night. Snow Hunter brought his adopted father to visit our hut. His name is Pethakaluns, which means "Thunder Arrow." Snow Hunter urged Thunder Arrow to tell a story.

Thunder Arrow lit his pipe with a coal from the fire. When he began to talk, Snow Hunter interpreted his story for Thomas and me.

Long ago a turtle, *takwax*, was lying in a great body of water. The water was the whole universe.

Slowly *takwax* raised his back. When the water ran off him, his dry shell became the earth.

In the middle of this dry earth grew a tree. The first man sprouted from the tree's foot. Then the first woman grew from the tip of the tree when it bent over and touched the ground.

Thus was the beginning of the world.

I asked Snow Hunter if he believed that the world really began this way.

He answered me simply, saying that different peoples have different dreams. This is the dream of his people, so he dreams it also.

I imagine it is the end of Fifth Month now, or the beginning of Sixth.

Another rainy evening. Snow Hunter visited, and we helped White Owl prepare plants for a special medicine. She urged us to remove the dirt as carefully as possible from the roots of the plant. Then she showed Thomas how to stir the brew.

Snow Hunter explained that it must be stirred in the direction that the sun travels. Then he told me that White Owl was giving the medicine to a man whose illness was caused by witchcraft.

Thomas asked who the witch was.

Snow Hunter said that no one knows for sure. But the victim's pain is the pain caused by a witch's curse.

I have never entertained belief in witches. But now that I live in this world, it seems something to reflect upon.

I have never believed that trees and plants have spirits, or that one should stir medicine in the direction the sun travels.

I consider all these customs now. I know they are not the truth as *we* know it, Papa.

But here is another truth: When thee lives close to a different people, it is hard not to dream what they dream.

Today we prepared for a celebration in the Big House.

Little Cloud and I worked on our deerskin garments. I sewed shell beads onto mine. Little Cloud embroidered a beautiful pattern on hers with porcupine quills dyed different colors.

Tonight all gathered in the Big House.

Two fires burned, filling the air with the scent of red cedar wood. The wind blew through the end doors, making shadows dance on the wooden walls.

A man wearing a bearskin appeared in the firelight. He wore a mask and carried a turtle-shell rattle and a stick.

The children were frightened. Thomas clutched my hand as the bear-man sacrificed tobacco and meat in the fire.

But when the bear-man led the group in dancing and singing, Thomas became enraptured. I did not want him to join in, for I know Quakers must never dance or sing in public, but I could not stop him, Papa. He joined the others and moved his little body as if he were all Indian.

I must confess, Papa, that my own eyes closed, my body swayed in the firelight, and I felt a strange, deep joy. Was this sinful, Papa? Or was it a visitation of the Holy Spirit?

I know we Quakers were given our name because we were mocked for quaking and trembling under the power of God. Is this dancing so different?

Papa, I had a dream of thee last night. Thee was at Meeting with Mother, Eliza, and Baby Will, and thee was grieving for me and Thomas. I woke up in tears, and I have felt thy presence all day. Please, Papa, do not grieve. I can stand my own tears, but thine are too much for me to bear.

The days are very long now, and all the trees are in full leaf and the wild roses are in bloom. Winter is fading even from memory. Is the farmland coming alive with the golden warmth, too, Papa? Bees and butterflies winging about? Baby Will walking? Are there new baby pigs?

Warm, lovely night. I write by candlelight as Thomas sleeps on our bed of deerskins.

Snow Hunter and other young men are having a ceremony to prepare to go hunting tomorrow. I hear their drumming coming from in front of the longhouse. Women cannot attend the ceremony. But I can see Snow Hunter in my mind, dancing in the firelight. Forgive me, Papa, but I think of him often.

Dear Papa, I remember last year when the piglets were born. Thee, Thomas, and I stayed up all night to help Curly give birth. Remember how she finally snored while they drank her milk, and we laughed so hard, we cried. Then Mother gave us sweet cornbread and thee thanked God for the gift of the little pigs.

It is good we didn't know of our impending separation that happy night, Papa. Our hearts could not have borne the thought. But please know now that Thomas and I are well, and mysteriously, sometimes we feel quite content.

Today two young boys came to our hut to play with Thomas. They are Running Deer and Little Bear.

White Owl served dried venison and smoked fish and corncakes. Then the boys played a sort of dice game with flat buttons made of bone. They counted their points with beans, but they kept scattering them, ruining their numbers.

Finally, I brought out my ink and paper and copied their scores. The boys stared with wonder as I wrote down each of their Indian names, sounding them out.

At the end of the night, they both wanted to take the score sheet with them. They drew sticks, and Little Bear got to keep the paper.

Their curiosity and interest has led me to wonder if perhaps I should teach English to the camp children.

I will ask Snow Hunter when he returns from his hunting trip. I worry about Snow Hunter roaming the wilderness. What if backwoodsmen should mistake him for an enemy?

Snow Hunter still gone.

Yesterday afternoon, Little Cloud and White Owl built a large fire. Then White Owl brought out a wooden doll about a foot long. She put red paint on its face and attached it to a stick. Then she stuck the stick into the earth.

Soon guests began to arrive. Each spoke to the doll. They called her *nuham*, which Thomas tells me means "grandmother."

As soon as it grew dark, dancing and singing began. The doll was passed from hand to hand as the young men and women danced.

Thomas and I watched them from the entrance of the *wigwam*, the hut. Little Cloud beckoned us to join them. Before I could stop him, Thomas threw himself into the dance. And suddenly, Papa, before I knew it, I was dancing, too! I had not intended to, but a joy came over me that prompted me to join them. I moved my feet and head and arms to the rhythm of the drums. Papa, I confess this with great guilt — I love to dance. I felt I was one with the music, the night, and my fellow dancers. Can thee ever forgive me?

We danced for a long time. After everyone took their leave, and Thomas and I lay down on our bed, my heart pounded. I could still hear the drumming and singing in my head.

When I woke this early morning, everything was quiet. The doll was gone, and the ground was swept clean. All trace of our sin had vanished.

Very hot day. Snow Hunter is not back. The men returned without him. I asked where he was. But I could not interpret their answer. Neither could Thomas.

What a terrible thing not to understand. I must learn more Lenape words.

Even hotter today. I made fishnets with Little Cloud and White Owl. We wove the nets with thread from wild hemp. As we worked, I longed to learn of Snow Hunter's whereabouts. Finally

I decided to use my copybook to ask my question.

First I drew a man's face with an eagle painted on his cheek. Then I cupped my hands over my eyes and turned my head from side to side, as if to say, "Where is he?"

White Owl and Little Cloud seemed confused, until Thomas piped up in plain English, "Where is Snow Hunter?"

Little Cloud laughed and gestured toward the trees. She pretended to shoot an arrow.

I laughed then, too. It seems they have been learning English from us faster than I have been learning Lenape from them. And I laughed because Snow Hunter is safe; he is still hunting in the forest.

"*Wishi. Wulelemil*," I said to her.

Good. Wonderful.

Many shad were swimming up the river today. A group of boys went fishing. Two set out in a canoe with one end of a long net. Others, including Thomas, stood on the shore, holding the other end of the net.

Those in the canoe pulled the net through the water, while those on shore pulled it also. By morning's end, they had captured at least one hundred fish.

In the afternoon, Little Cloud and I cleaned and prepared our share of the catch. We pegged each fish to a board, then cooked them in front of the fire.

Today we dried and smoked a great number of fish, so they could be stored and eaten later.

Snow Hunter returned in the late afternoon!

Thomas ran joyfully to meet him. But when the two approached me, I pretended to be very calm, only saying, "*Hah*."

"*Hah*," he said in return.

I was roasting meat on a spit. I asked if he was hungry.

He nodded and sat.

White Owl and Little Cloud joined us, and we all ate in happy silence, "a living silence," as Quaker Friends say.

I am grateful for Snow Hunter's safe return.

Tonight Snow Hunter invited Thomas and me to come with him to fish by torchlight.

Embraced by the warm, dark air, we sat in his *muxul*, or canoe, as he speared several large fish. Then Thomas and I held a small net as Snow Hunter silently paddled us up the river. We caught quite a number this way.

We worked in whispers as our light glowed upon the calm waters. A warm, lovely night, Papa. Indeed, I felt as if heaven had gathered us three and caught us in *its* net.

Today Thomas and Snow Hunter made fish-hooks of dried bird claws and harpoons from deer antlers. While they worked, White Owl, Little Cloud, and I tanned deerskins.

White Owl removed all the hair from the hides with a stone scraper. Little Cloud and I mashed the brains and rubbed them into the skin. Tomorrow the brains will be scraped off and the skins will be washed. Then we will rub each skin with a bone to make it soft.

Papa, these are some of the things we make from nature:

brooms from bird feathers
water dippers from gourds
buckets from bark
bowls from wood of the sassafras tree
cups from seashells
pots from clay
chisels from beaver teeth
rattles from turtle shells

red paint from the juice of wild crabapple

black paint from sumac mixed with black walnut bark

We are attached to the earth by a thousand threads.

Last night I dreamed that white bears came into the camp and started smashing our heads with clubs till our brains ran out. I woke up, screaming. White Owl rubbed my back with grease, then purified our hut with red-cedar smoke to chase away the bad spirits.

Am I now dreaming the dreams of the Lenape?

Today Snow Hunter, Thomas, and I went into the forest. Snow Hunter studied the trees, and he stopped before a tall hickory. He made an offering of tobacco to thank the spirit of the tree. Then he cut down a small branch.

When we returned to camp, he used his flint knife to remove the bark from the branch. Then he split the branch from end to end and hollowed out both halves. Finally he made a row of little holes in the wood.

Several times we asked him what he was doing, but he only smiled. When he joined the two halves together with pine pitch and wrapped them with deerskin, we saw that he had made a musical instrument that looked like a flute. He told us it is called an *ahpikon*.

When Thomas begged Snow Hunter to play for us, he nodded and said simply, "Someday."

Then he put the *ahpikon* in his belt and left.

All the while that we were together, I wanted to tell Snow Hunter my dream — of the white bears beating us — for I know he sees great meaning in such dreams. But something would not allow me to tell him. The horror of it all was too great. I would rather it be forgotten and never spoken of again.

Papa, remember the question in the Gospel of Luke: "Who is my neighbor?"

I think of that question as I sit near Thomas who sleeps on our bed of deerskins. I hear an owl call in the night air, and Little One coo from his cradleboard.

I think of thee and Mother, Eliza, and Baby Will, and I think how strange to be *here*. What for, Papa? To learn about those who are different from us? To learn something that few English people know — a quick and lively knowledge of those some would call "savage?"

Papa, the Lenape are my neighbors. Sitting here peacefully, I feel a current of God's love running through this life, though He is known here by a different name.

Snow Hunter tells me the Lenape believe that corn was first dropped out of the sky from the mouth of a crow. Today we all worked together, harvesting our crop. Then we roasted the ears in their husks until their kernels popped off.

Tomorrow we begin pounding the kernels night and day into cornmeal.

Tonight I sewed skirts with Little Cloud and White Owl. As we used awls to bore holes through deerskin, I heard music from outside. Flute music.

Little Cloud and White Owl glanced at each other, then smiled at me. When Thomas started to go outside, White Owl gently grabbed him by the arm.

She looked at me and motioned for *me* to go outside instead.

I felt suddenly nervous. I wrapped a deerskin shawl around my shoulders, then stepped out into the dark.

Snow Hunter sat in the moonlight, playing his *ahpikon*. I sat near him and listened to his haunting, lovely song. Was he playing for me?

When he finished, I asked, "Who taught thee to play?"

"The eagle," he answered.

When I asked if that was the name of one who lived in our camp, he smiled and shook his head. Then he explained. Three years ago when he was fourteen, he went alone into the deep forest in search of a vision. He neither ate nor drank for many days. He only prayed that a good spirit would be his guardian.

On the seventh day, when he was near collapse, he saw an eagle in the sky. The eagle talked to him and told him that he would always look after him, that he would turn him into a great hunter and teach him to play music.

Snow Hunter returned home after his eagle vision. From that day on, he could hunt better than anyone else, and he could play the *ahpikon*.

He said that the eagle was his guardian. This is why he tattooed one on his cheek.

I reminded him that his eagle had visited my dream, that he had covered Thomas with his great wings.

He smiled and told me that was the reason he had taken me to see Thomas, for he knew my dream was sending *him* a message.

I told him that I believe all things in nature bear the mark of their Maker. The eagle, the owl, and the wind.

We sat silently for a long moment, understanding that we are not so different really. We remained in this living silence until I began to shiver. Then he told me he must leave, and he lightly brushed my hair with his hand.

"*Wanishi*," I said. I am thankful.

All day Snow Hunter's song was with me.

In the morning, Little Cloud strapped Little One to her back, and went berry hunting with Thomas and me. We filled our baskets with strawberries. Suddenly the sky grew black. Then thunder shook the ground and rain began to fall.

Little Cloud led us to a rock shelter where we waited while the rain poured down and lightning lit up the forest.

The sound of the thunder was the loudest I have ever heard. Little One did not cry at all, but I confess Thomas and I were much alarmed.

Little Cloud tried to soothe our terror by stroking our hair and smiling at us and pretending not to be frightened.

When the storm finally passed, I was so grateful to her, I held her arm all the way back to our camp.

Snow Hunter came to dinner. When Thomas told him about our adventure, he said that the thunder was made by Thunder Beings. "They are huge birds with human heads who shoot lightning bolts from their bows," he said.

"Really?" Thomas's eyes grew wide. "Is thee telling the truth?"

"Yes," said Snow Hunter. "The sharp, crackling thunder is made by young Thunder Beings. Low, rumbling sounds by old ones."

Thomas looked at me, as if asking me to verify this information. I only shrugged and smiled.

I know that Quakers do not believe in Thunder Beings, but in that moment, listening to Snow Hunter, I could not banish them thoroughly from my mind.

Hearty dinner tonight. Beans boiled with bear grease and fresh turkey meat broiled on coals. After we ate, Snow Hunter, White Owl, Little Cloud, and I passed the time in silence. Now and again, one murmured about the deeds of the day, but mostly, we listened to the sounds of twilight, the crickets, and cooing night birds.

Our days and nights are getting cooler. Late summer weather. Today I helped Little Cloud and White Owl gather acorns. Later we roasted them to remove their bad taste, then pounded them and added them to our cornbread.

While we worked outside, Snow Hunter stopped by to bid us hello. After he left, White Owl smiled at me and made a sign to Little Cloud to indicate that Snow Hunter and I were a pair. Then Little Cloud rocked her arms as if she were rocking a baby.

Do they think that Snow Hunter and I will be married? I was so astonished, I quickly finished off my work and went inside to lie down.

I am only thirteen! But Lenape girls sometimes marry as young as thirteen or fourteen, I
have learned. What am I to think?

I am in a state of confusion over Little Cloud's
gestures about Snow Hunter and myself.

This morning, I followed discreetly when
Thomas went into the forest to help Snow
Hunter and the other men make a canoe. Soon
they are going on an expedition downriver to
sell their animal skins to Canadian traders who
live in Bethlehem.

They cut down a huge tulip poplar, then
burned and scraped the trunk, hollowing it out
to hold eight men.

While they worked, I watched Snow Hunter
from afar. He seemed totally engaged in his task,
without entertaining any thought of me.

He looked very handsome and strong in the
sunlight.

It is strange. But now I do not feel as though I am writing for Papa. I feel as though I am writing for myself.

What should happen if I were to marry Snow Hunter? Though Snow Hunter was born an Englishman, he is definitely Indian now. If he were my husband, would Papa's Quaker love still embrace him?

If I were his wife, I fear I could never return home, for he does not seem to have the slightest inclination to live among the English again. I would have to live here always. And what of Thomas? I think if thee asked him today, Thomas would say he would like to grow up to be just like Snow Hunter.

If Papa, Mother, Eliza, and Baby Will were not on this earth, I would welcome such a fate among these people. Indeed, sometimes I feel that White Owl, Little Cloud, and Little One are my new family.

But I cannot stand to think that Thomas and I might be forever exiled from our loved ones back home. Help me, God.

Snow Hunter came around tonight to say good-bye, for he and his party embark tomorrow morning on their journey.

He asked to speak with me alone, so I accompanied him into the moonlight. He stood very close to me and touched my hair. He whispered, "Snow Bird captures the Snow Hunter."

My heart nearly stopped. He planted a soft kiss upon my forehead, then held me to him, and I could feel both our hearts beating, and I wanted to be his wife. He gently let me go. Then he whispered, "*Wanishi*," and he left me alone in the dark.

I love him.

The whole village saw the men off today. Eight of them, including Snow Hunter, embarked in their canoe down the river to sell their skins and furs.

Before they left, Snow Hunter spoke kind words to me.

"I will see you in a dream," he said. "And you will see me."

"Yes," I said. "Good be to thee."

He silently handed me a string of white shell beads, or *wampum*. Then he gave Thomas his *ahpikon* and asked him to keep it until he returns.

The canoe pushed off, and the men moved silently away from us, like the yellow leaves floating down the river.

Only once did Snow Hunter glance back at me. I waved and he smiled, radiant in the early autumn sunlight.

My heart is heavy, but they will be back in two weeks, the Great Spirit willing.

Little Cloud and I made new fish lines today from hand-twisted bark. Then we sewed rushes together for new floor mats and repaired torn sleeves on our deerskin robes.

All the time, I felt an emptiness without Snow

Hunter in our camp. At the same time, I am content with the certain knowledge of his love for me.

If I marry him, I will persuade him to take Thomas and me home. Perhaps we could all be together at the farm for a long visit. Papa and Mother would both like him. He speaks plainly and honestly, and he seems to have great courage and loving-kindness.

I helped White Owl with a healing today. Her patient was an old woman, older than herself. She will not die, White Owl says, because when I placed the healing roots in water, they did not sink.

We also boiled corn tassel into tea. White Owl will give it to a mother with a colicky baby. Perhaps this would be a good remedy for Baby Will. We also boiled cottonwood bark to make an ointment for sore limbs. White Owl has great knowledge of the natural world — does that not bring her close to God's truth?

My mind and heart constantly wander to thoughts of Snow Hunter. Sometimes I imagine I hear the song he played for me.

Thomas and I collected wild strawberries today and gathered nuts. Little Cloud crushed the strawberries and made a balm for herself and for me, too. With hand signs, she explained that the berries would make our skin softer. I fear Quakers would not forgive me my vanity, but the truth is — if my skin is made softer by Little Cloud's balm, I would not mind.

Then White Owl ground the nuts. We will use their milky fluid as a flavoring.

Snow Hunter has been gone nine days. I need wait only a few more.

Last night I could not sleep. I realized in the dark, cold silence of night that our Society of

Friends would never give Snow Hunter and me a certificate of marriage. I would be turned out in the most shameful manner. My sins would be far worse than just unruly conduct or marrying one not in our religious society or being tempted by finery and pride in appearance.

Far worse than all this, I will have joined my heart to that of a heathen.

Am I brave enough to follow my own still, small voice? Would Mother and Papa still love me?

All day my mind has been tortured — one minute I grieve that I will most certainly be turned out of the Society — the next minute, I angrily fight for myself. My best defense: Would the great William Penn scorn me if he were still alive? I think he would not. I will try to find peace in this certainty.

Our men are hourly expected. Perhaps they will return near twilight. I will be nervous when I hear they are coming, and tremble for the sight of Snow Hunter. I imagine his party will return through the forest from the river. I imagine Thomas will run to greet him — and persuade him to come to our fire at once for dinner.

Little Cloud and White Owl will broil venison, and I will make corncakes. After we have eaten, perhaps he will light a pipe and offer the smoke to the Great Spirit for his party's safe return. Then perhaps he will speak Lenape to White Owl and Little Cloud, and kindly interpret each word for me and Thomas, and thus he will tell us all of the success of his journey and describe the birds and the wild animals and the weather.

Then while all the others sleep, perhaps he will play his flute for me alone.

I have waited all night and still Snow Hunter has not returned. It is dawn now. The sun shines on the leaves. They are turning even more brilliant colors. I long to share the autumn with him.

The men did not come back yesterday, nor today. For three days, Thomas and Little Bear have climbed tall trees near the river to keep watch.

This morning, White Owl burned red cedar to dispel bad spirits. She indicated that a dream has brought pain to her heart, but she would not say what that dream was.

A windy, rainy day.
Still the men do not return. Feeling a strange sort of dread, I lay in our hut, listening to the rain, and I pray for the skin over the doorway to

be suddenly pulled aside and for Snow Hunter to appear, wet, safe, and well from his journey.

A messenger from the Indian camp over the hill came today. He spoke first to White Owl and the others, and though I could not understand his words, I could see his news was bad, for everyone was clearly anguished.

I begged him to explain to me and was grateful to learn that he could speak a little English. Thus I heard that a party of Indians was attacked some days ago on the river by English soldiers. He does not know if the Indians were our men or not.

All of us gathered in the longhouse to pray and offer tobacco for the safe return of Snow Hunter and his party.

Afterward women came to me in anxious search of answers. At first, they gestured with their hands, I could not interpret their meaning. But gradually I came to understand that they think I have special knowledge of this situation because the English are my people. Some even question whether or not Thomas and I should be sent out from the camp — they wonder if the soldiers are murdering on our behalf.

Still our men have not returned. We are desperate for fresh news, fearing they may have been murdered by the hands of white men. A watch is kept night and day. To raise our courage, White Owl prays constantly and burns red cedar.

Word arrived that bands of English soldiers are now scouring the forests for Indian camps. I think of the attack on the Conestogas in Lancaster and shudder with terror.

Now all are lying quietly in their huts. I keep awake, listening for the drunken cries of a mob. My fear reminds me of when I lay in bed at home, waiting for the Indians to attack. All terror is alike.

Today the women, children, and old men gathered whatever might be used as weapons — old knives, bows and arrows, even sticks and stones. We will take the weapons and pack our essential things, flee our camp, and hide in the yellow autumn woods.

In the late afternoon, word came that the white men were only a few miles away. Panic set in. White Owl sought to calm everyone and urged us to pack very little and move quickly and quietly into the forest.

Our footfall was noisy though, as we stepped

over a crackling carpet of dead leaves. Finally, with relief, we arrived at a rock shelter that White Owl knows from her medicine hunts.

Now at the approach of dark, we eat nuts, dried deer meat, berries, and cornmeal. We are about fifteen women, twenty children, and a few old men.

As the cloak of chilly night falls over us, White Owl softly prays to the Great Spirit for protection. Little One whimpers. Little Cloud tries to console him, covering his small round face with kisses.

Clinging to Thomas, I am worn out with fear and pray for sleep.

A wet, windy dawn. Leaves whirl wildly as we all huddle together. Earlier, Little Cloud crept close to me and with her hands asked me why the white men want to kill them. I told her that they do not understand that the same light of humanity that is in them is also in her people. I told her that God means her no harm, and I beseeched Him to hide us all under the shadow of His wing. Though Little Cloud does not know much English, I felt she understood my tone. She pressed my arm as if *she* were comforting *me*.

The children are growing more fretful and restless by the hour. We do not have enough provisions, and many are shivering in the damp cold.

Sunlight illuminates yellow and orange leaves. The day is filled with an autumn glow, raising all our hopes and spirits. We wonder if perhaps the soldiers have come and gone from our camp. Perhaps our men have returned and are searching for us. White Owl says we should return home.

Such horror in sunlight. God mocking us. I shudder in the depths of my being. I have no words.

Dear God, why did Thy terrors turn against us? Why did Thee bring the soldiers down upon us? Why did Thee harm White Owl?

No one will tell me what has become of the Lenape. I cannot write. I have no heart and no faith.

20th of Tenth Month, 1764

For the first time in many months, I know the date. It is the twentieth day of Tenth Month. Thomas and I have re-entered time. And in this bitter world of time, everything seems rigid and unyielding.

Three days we have been lodged in this fort and strictly guarded. We have been scrubbed clean by unloving hands and dressed in scratchy wool clothing. Thomas mutely watches out the window, while I sit alone, trying to fight off the memory that tears at my soul like a lion: White Owl's red blood in the autumn light.

Over and over again, I am tortured by one thought: If I had told Snow Hunter my dream of the white bears attacking us, would we all be safe now? Would he have moved us all to safety, far away from the horror that stalked us?

21st of Tenth Month, 1764

I must record the sorrowful events of that sunny day.

When we returned to the still and quiet of our camp, everything was the same as we had left it. Within moments, we all resumed our daily activities in innocent hope that our fears of the white soldiers were unfounded.

Thomas and I began gathering corn. As we lost ourselves amidst the swaying, dusty stalks, they came. One English soldier, then another, then another, crashed through the tall stalks, their guns raised.

I grabbed Thomas and we ran to our hut. I whispered madly to him that whatever happened we must not reveal our true identity. Thus, we concealed ourselves under a bearskin and peered out from the shadowy entrance as the others were rounded up in the bright sunshine.

The soldiers began to bully White Owl, for she stood between them and the rest like a fierce guardian. When one bloated soldier called her an old witch and pushed her aside, she slipped and fell. Their party laughed. Little Cloud rushed to her mother's side with Little One in her arms — they mocked her and one of the soldiers spat on her.

I have never felt such rage before. It filled every cell of my being, every hair, bone, and bit of blood. I trembled, but I could not move, could not open my mouth, nor run forward, for

I thought White Owl would fare even more miserably for such a revelation.

Thomas, however, could not silently bear the cruelty of it. The Holy Spirit found pure expression in him as he ran screaming from our hut into the party of men and pummeled them with his little fists and bit them, and when they held him at bay, laughing, they heard his words: "Leave them alone!"

They knew at once he was English. They seized him, kicking and screaming, and then I was forced to come forward, to reveal myself and betray my friends. Lurching into the cruel sunshine, I cried for them to let him go. "He means no harm to thee! None of them means harm to thee!" I cried.

White Owl tried to crawl to me, but one man hit her with the butt of his rifle, and she fell on her face, bleeding. Then others grabbed me and tied my hands.

They forced Thomas and me to come with them. As we left, we heard screaming behind us, but could not see what happened. Then we smelled smoke and saw flames leaping above the trees.

In the hours of darkness that followed that hideous scene, I have imagined the worst and eat my heart in anguish, thinking my existence on Earth has brought pain and torment to those I have come to love as friends. I cannot stop the memory of White Owl's blood on the leaves in the bright sunshine. How the sunshine betrayed us.

22nd of Tenth Month, 1764

This morning Thomas and I were rousted from our beds and ushered out into a damp, gray day. Our captors have assigned us to several traders heading to the Moravian mission near Bethlehem. I asked the traders if they knew what had become of the Lenape camp, but they seemed not to know what I meant.

I still cannot forgive myself for bringing harm upon my friends.

23rd of Tenth Month, 1764

We are camped on a rise above the water. The traders seem oblivious to Thomas and myself. We have nothing to say to them. We simply do as they tell us. Now Thomas sleeps fitfully while I write.

24th of Tenth Month, 1764

We journeyed all day downriver, taking perhaps the very path taken by Snow Hunter and his party. When he came this way, did he hear the same birds singing? Did he see the same fish gliding beneath the surface of the water? Is his flesh now rotting somewhere in the scrub near this river?

25th of Tenth Month, 1764

Perhaps Snow Hunter escaped danger and made his way home on foot and has now returned to the camp and found White Owl recovered from her wounds. And perhaps the two of them have bundled all to safety beyond these dark forests.

26th of Tenth Month, 1764

Last night a dream told me that Snow Hunter has departed this life. In the dream, a poisonous green snake slithered through the summer forest, attacked him, then moved on to murder White Owl.

27th of Tenth Month, 1764

Bells chime from the mission bell house. We arrived here today. Neither of us had the strength to return the warmth extended to us by the Moravians. Reverend Beckwell's wife kindly led us to a clean room so that we could rest alone. Then a girl brought us warm soup and bread, but we have eaten little, for we are too weary and feel poorly.

Thomas lies on his cot shivering with fever. I must stop writing and comfort him.

28th of Tenth Month, 1764

Thomas and I both have fever.

29th of Tenth Month, 1764

Papa sat up all night with us and now sleeps in a chair between my bed and Thomas's bed. He arrived last night, after our candle was out. He came into the room with a lantern to look upon us. When I saw his bright face by the flame, I thought I was dreaming, and I began to tremble and said that we needed his help, we *all* desperately needed his help. Then I saw that he did not fade away, and I felt myself jolted back into my old world, and we grabbed one another, and a sleepy Thomas piled on Papa's back, and we all clung together as one great giant.

Now Papa sleeps, with one hand on Thomas's bed and one hand on my mine. His palms are up and his head is dropped back, as if he were thanking God Almighty.

30th of Tenth Month, 1764

We are well enough to travel. Today we will climb into Papa's wagon to journey back to our farm. He warned us that Mother, Eliza, and Baby Will might be nervous and emotional, and told us to forgive them. He said that neighbors might come by to stare at us, and they might ask painful questions, and we should forgive them also. I believe he is warning us thus because neither of us has spoken much, trapped as we are in our numb and weary silence.

31st of Tenth Month, 1764

Wrapped in a blanket, Thomas slept most of the journey while I stared at the maple trees. Their last yellow leaves made the day seem sunny, though it was not. Papa, unlike himself, hummed a tune.

When we arrived at our house, everything looked familiar, yet distant. When Mother tearfully embraced Thomas, he began to cry also; but when she embraced me, I was stiff and cold.

Eliza looked at us shyly, as if we were strangers, and Baby Will, too. In a way, I feel they are right — I *am* a stranger now.

At dinner, Thomas sat in Mother's lap and she fed him as if he were a baby. I stared at my plate without appetite, and Papa recommended that I go up to bed and rest.

Now, in the loft, I stare out the window at the twilight. Dear God, will I ever come home?

2nd of Eleventh Month, 1764

Today Lucy, Molly, and Jess Owen all came together to visit me. When I first laid eyes on Jess, I felt nothing, not even nervousness. Beside Snow Hunter, he seems very dull and youthful. I had nothing to say to any of them — not from shyness, but from despair. Finally they conversed only with one another as if I were not present.

3rd of Eleventh Month, 1764

Thomas and I went to our first Meeting today since we have been back. Papa was right. While we all sat in silence, I glimpsed many Friends staring at us as if we had returned from the dead. Afterwards, the children circled around us, craving knowledge of our terrible experiences.

6th of Eleventh Month, 1764

Neighbors still come by and inquire anxiously after us. They want to know what happened to us when the savages captured us, but I find it impossible to explain. How do I tell them that we went into the lions' den — and found tenderness and mercy. When I turn away, Papa tells them I do not wish to talk about it.

Thomas also feels disinclined to share our experience with others. I think he does not have the language to reflect upon its confusions, while I have not the heart.

7th of Eleventh Month, 1764

Wet, windy day. All the leaves are gone. I sit by the window, watching the rain. I am not of the mind to return to school. A terrible bitterness oppresses me, and often I must sit so as not to faint.

Mother keeps a constant, watchful eye on me and Thomas. She and Papa seem to think that I was tortured by the Indians and am not in my right mind.

I long to explain the truth to them. But I fear they would never understand.

8th of Eleventh Month, 1764

Tonight in the early evening, I heard Thomas playing the *aphikon*. He played the song Snow Hunter played for me.

I could not bear the agony of it, so I ran from the house into the dark woods and cursed God for the grief I had seen, the blood in the sunlight, the violence and rumor of slaughter.

By the time Papa found me, collapsed on the cold ground, night had fallen.

In the dark, he assured me that I was home, I was safe. He would not allow harm to come to me again. I could only lean against him, mute and trembling, unable to declare my true thoughts.

After he led me back to the house, I came up to the loft to write.

I have made a decision. I must give my diary to Papa. Long ago, in desperation, I began writing it for him. But then, to my amazement, a greater truth revealed itself to me and I began to write it for myself.

Now I fear that if I cannot share that self with him, I will never come home.

9th of Eleventh Month, 1764

Papa read my diary last night. He returned it this morning while I slept, leaving it beside my bed. He did not wake me to speak to me.

I fear he is ashamed to death that I am his daughter. He may want nothing more to do with me, for now he knows that I was willing to forsake my old life to marry and live forever with the Lenape.

10th of Eleventh Month, 1764

Papa went into the fields before daylight and has not returned all day. I imagine that he is overwhelmed by his wrath and thus is afraid to speak to me.

11th of Eleventh Month, 1764

Papa spent the day alone in the fields again. But before my candle was out, he returned. Now I wait anxiously for him to come and talk to me, but he has not. I hear him climb into his bed. His candle goes out. I feel dreadfully alone.

12th of Eleventh Month, 1764

Papa gone all day again. Finally, after dark, he returned. He did not look at me all through supper, though I scarcely ever took my eyes off him.

After the little ones had been put to bed, he asked me to follow him outside. When we stepped out into the evening, he said that he had spent all day in silence, asking for God's guidance.

In a low voice, he told me that my diary had taught him that I had stood in the light. But this is all he said! And when I waited for more, it was not forthcoming. He went back inside, and with a confused heart, I followed, then came upstairs.

13th of Eleventh Month, 1764

Tonight I talked to Papa and Mother about our way of life in the Lenape camp. I recalled tender moments with Snow Hunter, White Owl, and Little Cloud.

Thomas heard me and came down from the loft and told about how we danced the Doll Dance and how we fished and how the Great Turtle made the world.

I fear Mother was a bit horrified, for she spoke very little and finally declared she had a headache and must retire. Papa kept a steady, concentrated gaze upon us, as if he were listening to us and praying for guidance at the same time.

I long for Papa and Mother to understand the truths I have learned. But perhaps I must always carry them by myself. As I write this, my heart beats anxiously at the thought of such loneliness.

14th of Eleventh Month, 1764

This morning Papa told Thomas and me that it would be better if we did not share our stories in Meeting or at school. He said that the two worlds of English and Indian are still far apart, and only a few people would understand our journey. He added that Mother was very upset by what we had told her. He asked us to be gentle with her.

15th of Eleventh Month, 1764

When Molly and Lucy visited again today, they asked how I was able to bear my life with the filthy Indians.

I could not answer them.

Later, after they had left, I offered to help Mother with supper, but she said she did not need my help. I tried to read, but I grew desperately lonely, knowing that Mother is repulsed by our experience.

So I went out to the fields and looked at the sky, and I begged God to take my life. I will never belong here again. I have no home. I lay on the ground to be close to the scent of the earth and lost all sense of time, until Papa found me.

I calmly confessed to him that I did not want to live for I was desperately lonely and could not bear Mother's wrath against me.

He took my face between his hands and said, "Thee learned to open thy heart to those who are different from thee, Caty. That is why thee stood in the light. But such learning is very lonely and cannot be taught to others, for thee had to suffer greatly to uncover such truth."

When he said this, I broke for the first time since the attack on the Lenape camp and collapsed in a terrible grief. Papa held me tightly as tears flooded forth and my tongue was released. I told him that my friends had no outward sign of wealth, but their lives outshone those of many Christians, and that Snow Hunter was not unlike him or me — and White Owl and Little Cloud and Little One, that we were all part of the same family.

Then I wept with loud cries against his shoulder for the terrible sorrow of it all.

He held me tighter and said, "Thee must pray for thy red friends, Caty. For the same loving Spirit who loves thee loves them, though they know Him by another name. Thee must know that we are all always in God's embrace, whether we are alive or have departed this earth."

16th of Eleventh Month, 1764

All day Thomas and I helped Mother with chores and tended to Baby Will who walks easily on his own now and pries into everything. I was more cheerful with Mother, and she seemed relieved. Perhaps it is I who will have to move closer to her and reassure her that all is well.

I feel better since talking to Papa, but I do not know if I shall ever be able to return to school.

17th of Eleventh Month, 1764

Rain taps against the roof. Thomas sleeps, exhausted from helping Papa and Cousin Ezra chop wood all day.

As usual I cannot sleep. I am still melancholy. How will I live without ever knowing the fate of White Owl, Little Cloud, Little One, and Snow Hunter?

18th of Eleventh Month, 1764

Weather raw and cool. Mother and I quilted all afternoon, then cleaned iron candlesticks. We spoke very little, still miles apart in our thoughts and feelings. But at least we were together, and several times she smiled lovingly at me. Tonight I felt her warm gaze upon me as I gave Thomas a reading lesson before the fire.

Mother and Papa both laughed with relief when Thomas asked if he could learn to divide the long numbers. I imagine Mother perceives that Thomas is adapting back to his life, and will soon forget his "savage" experience.

I fear it is very different for me.

20th of Eleventh Month, 1764

Thomas returned to school today, but I was disinclined to do the same. Mother kindly allows me to stay home.

21st of Eleventh Month, 1764

Today at Meeting, a Friend quoted William Penn: "They that love beyond the world cannot be separated by it."

I do not imagine that William Penn was talking about the sort of love I have known, but 'tis strange that when I left Meeting, I saw an eagle flying high above the trees. I whispered, "I will always love thee, Snow Hunter."

Somehow I believe I was heard, for the great bird circled twice, then dipped gracefully down toward me before he glided away into the infinite.

A knowingness flooded my heart, and I felt that someday, somewhere on this earth or beyond it, we will meet again.

Wanishi.

Epilogue

Catharine Carey Logan did not return to school that year. She felt too estranged from her friends after her life among the Lenape. The following year, her mother died of yellow fever, and she was thenceforth compelled to stay home and care for Eliza and Baby Will. Her father, however, educated her himself. Once the younger children were grown, she became a teacher, and taught in Philadelphia.

Catharine never married. She taught impoverished children throughout the period of the Revolutionary War. After the war, she devoted herself to the abolition of slavery and traveled throughout the South, urging southern Quakers to give up their slaves. Her experiences with the Lenape had taught her that all people deserve equal respect and treatment.

Thomas Logan was likewise profoundly affected by his experiences with the Lenape

Indians. After the Revolutionary War, he helped represent Indian interests when the Six Nations made treaties with the United States government. He also helped establish centers where farming and other skills were taught to eastern Indians who had been forced to live on reservations.

For many years, Thomas inquired after the small Lenape band with whom he and his sister had lived — he calculated that they must have had their camp on the northern branch of the Susquehanna River. No one seemed to know the fate of White Owl, Little Cloud, Little One, and their people. Moravian missionaries assured him, though, that if they had survived the attack of the soldiers, they most likely had migrated west over the Appalachian Mountains to join many of their people who at that time lived peacefully in the Ohio Valley.

From the Moravians, Thomas also gathered information about a boy who had lived near Pittsburgh, Pennsylvania, and had been captured by the Lenape in 1756. The boy's name was John McCloud. As he was nine years old at the time of his capture, he would have been seventeen in 1764, the approximate age of Snow Hunter. According to various sources, John McCloud was killed by soldiers in the fall of 1764.

Life in America
in 1763

Historical Note

Many of the early settlers of America were members of newly formed religious groups from Europe who had come seeking a place to live and to practice their faith freely. The Quakers were a Protestant group that had formed in England in the 1600s. Though rooted in Christianity, the early Quakers taught that all people in the world, regardless of their religion, were illuminated by an inner light. They believed that this light was part of God and it would help guide a person to do what was right.

The early Quakers met for worship in meetinghouses or in someone's home. Their form of worship was very simple. There was no singing, no sermon or communion. The "Friends," as Quakers call themselves, sat in silence. During the silence, any Friend was allowed to share a prayer or message with the group.

During the 1650s and the 1660s, the first Quakers who came to America from England were persecuted by the Puritans. Over time, they gained acceptance, and in 1682, an aristocratic English Quaker named William Penn was given a tract of land by King Charles II. The land became the colony of Pennsylvania (named after Penn by the king). Penn declared it a "Holy Experiment," as he wanted its government to rule justly, according to Quaker truths. He named its major city "Philadelphia" which means the "City of Brotherly Love."

When Penn came to Pennsylvania, the Lenni Lenape (who were called the Delaware Indians by the early settlers) were an Indian tribe who held their ancestral lands in New York, New Jersey, Delaware, and Pennsylvania.

Penn and the early Quakers insisted that the Lenape Indians of Pennsylvania be treated fairly. Thus, for the next fifty years, there was peace between white settlers and the Lenape. One of Penn's treaties, however, did not serve the Indians well. He had made an agreement to buy land from them west of the Delaware River, the size of which was to be determined as the distance a man could walk in a day and a half. Both sides understood this to mean about thirty miles. However, it was not until 1737 that the "Walking Purchase" was carried out by Penn's descendants, who had no concern for the welfare of the Indians. They cut a road through the wilderness and hired professional runners to "walk" at a run. Thus, the area covered stretched to sixty miles instead of thirty, and included virtually all of the remaining eastern territory of the Indians.

Quakers were reluctant to enforce the "Walking Purchase," for they loathed robbing the Indians of their ancestral territory. Non-Quakers, however, demanded that the treaty be honored. Thus, the "Walking Purchase" (or the "Extravagant Day's Walk," as it was sometimes called) contributed to the disintegration of harmony between settlers and Indians.

Relations went from bad to worse. In the 1750s, when the French and English fought over the land in the Ohio Valley, they both treated the Indians unfairly. English and French traders bribed and cheated them, stole their lands, and insulted their leaders. The Lenape finally chose to side with the French as they were angry with the English for building forts on their land. Further, the French had convinced them that the English were planning to make them slaves.

In an effort to end the French and Indian War, the English eventually met with the Indians in a series of treaty meetings and promised protection and compensation for ancestral lands.

However, when the war ended in the early 1760s, the English failed to keep their promises. In despair, the Indians tried to capture English posts. Later when they attacked families of the Scotch-Irish frontiersmen, all Quaker pleas for a peaceful relationship with them went unheeded. In fact, other settlers became angry at the Quakers for trying to protect the Indians.

Finally, in December of 1763, a vigilante mob called the "Paxton boys" decided to teach the Indians a lesson. They rounded up and brutally murdered members of the peaceful Conestoga tribe of Lancaster County.

For the next year, the Lenape and other eastern tribes fought with the settlers until, in the early fall of 1764, English troops destroyed most of the remaining Lenape villages in Pennsylvania. At that time the Indians were forced to return their captives taken during and after the French and Indian War. A number of captives, however, had formed meaningful bonds with the Indians and did not want to return.

After they were defeated, many of the surviving Lenape moved west into Ohio, then later into Indiana, Kansas, and Oklahoma.

By the end of the eighteenth century, Pennsylvania Quakers were little involved with government matters. Still, eastern Indian tribes considered them friends and asked them to represent their interests when they signed treaties with the new United States. Those Quakers who tried to protect the rights of the Indians appeared to have believed in the philosophy expressed by William Penn a century earlier: "Force subdues but love gains."

The pious Quakers adhered to strict rules within their society, even in matters of fashion. Women wore long, simple high-necked dresses with plain bonnets. Men wore short, fitted pants known as breeches, jackets with little adornment, and the traditional flat-brimmed hat.

Lenape women and girls dressed in fringed buckskin skirts, or tepethuns, *made from animal hides. Lenape men and boys wore long pieces of deerskin folded over a belt known as a* sàkutàkàn, *or breechcloth. The breechcloth was worn alone in warm weather and accompanied by animal skin pants during the winter. Both men and women decorated their clothing with feathers, shells, and the quills of porcupines, and wore moccasins on their feet.*

169

Many Quakers lived in the lush countryside of the Delaware Valley and made homes on farms similar to the one pictured here. Every day, except Sunday, was filled with chores. Women and girls cooked, washed, and sewed, while men and boys planted and harvested crops and tended the farm animals.

Many Quaker children were unable to go to school every day because lessons were often interrupted by seasonal harvesting and demanding household chores. This drawing depicts a young girl studying geography in a Quaker Friends school. Quaker Friends schools still exist today.

The Friends meetinghouse provided a religious sanctuary where the Quakers could worship together. Their reverent society emphasized the importance of a direct relationship with God, thriftiness, modest social behavior, and unity.

William Penn, a leader of the Pennsylvania Quakers, met with the early colonists to discuss his hopes to keep peace with their Lenape neighbors.

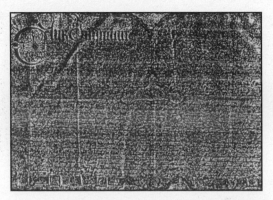

This actual Lenape deed, from July 15, 1682, is for land in Buck's County, Pennsylvania, that was negotiated by William Penn's agent William Markham. Signatures and distinguishing marks of Indian leaders can be seen at the bottom.

This painting depicts William Penn with members of the Lenape, Shawnee, and Susquehannock tribes. The "Walking Purchase" treaty that Penn signed with them stated that the land he purchased would extend as far as a person could walk in a day and a half. However, fifty years later, when the treaty was carried out, non-Quaker colonists cheated the Indians by using skilled runners who covered twice that distance.

La-Pa-Win-Soe was a powerful Lenape chief who signed the "Walking Purchase" treaty. Indian tribes in the Delaware Valley looked to their leaders for guidance and honor.

The Lenape were remarkably skilled at utilizing the natural world. Longhouses are one of the best examples of their handiwork. Men and boys would uproot young trees, called saplings, curve them into frames, and cover them with strips of bark. These homes provided the Lenape with comfortable shelter throughout the year.

The interior of the longhouse was quite large. Wooden benches used for beds lined the walls; storage shelves were stacked with baskets overhead; and drying herbs and corn hung from the ceiling. Lenape women cooked, sewed, and performed many daily duties inside the longhouse.

The Lenape were egalitarian, and women played a vital role in society. Gardens and houses were considered their property, and family inheritance was traced through the mother.

Trunks of large trees were used to make dugout canoes so the Lenape could travel vast distances swiftly by river. The inside of trees were burned, and the charred wood was scraped away with stone tools to hollow out the interior.

THE
Soveraignty and Goodness of
GOD,
Together with the Faithfulness of His Promises Displayed:
BEING A
NARRATIVE
Of the Captivity and Restauration of
Mrs. *Mary Rowlandson.*

Commended by her, to all that desire to know the Lords Doings to, & Dealings with her; especially to her dear Children and Relations.

Written by her own Hand, for her private Use, and now made Publick at the earnest Desire of some Friends, and for the Benefit of the Afflicted.

The Second Edition.

Carefully Corrected, and Purged from abundance of Errors which escaped in the former Impression

Captive narratives began to appear as early as the mid-1600s. This narrative written by Mary Rowlandson was published in 1682. Captive narratives such as this one provided valuable insight into the Indians' way of life and their treatment of captives.

It was not uncommon for captives to feel bewildered and displaced when they returned to their native communities.

CANDLE MAKING

You will need: Several chunks of paraffin wax, an 8-inch length of candlewick, a small empty can, and a saucepan.

1. Fill the saucepan with about 2 inches of water and heat it over a low heat on the stove.

2. Put a few chunks of paraffin wax into the can, and place the can into the water.

3. Let the paraffin melt.

4. Slowly lower the wick down into the liquid wax.

5. Slowly lift the wick out. Hold it until the wax begins to cool and get solid.

6. Repeat steps 4 and 5, over and over, until the candle is the size you want.

7. Hang the candle by the wick end to cool.

8. Trim the extra wick.

(Warning: Paraffin wax catches fire if it gets too hot. Drips of hot wax can burn your skin. Ask an adult to help you with this craft.)

For the colonists, candle making was a tedious chore involving tallow, or hard animal fat. Here is a simple candle making recipe using paraffin wax, which replaced tallow in the late 1800s.

THE WOLF, THE WOLF

TUM-MAY, TUM-MAY	The wolf, the wolf
LUK-KWEE-XEEN,	he growls,
LUK-KWEE-XEEN	he growls
OO-CHAY, OO-CHAY	The fly, the fly
WEE-TAO-KAH	his ears
TUM-MAY, TUM-MAY	The wolf, the wolf
LUK-KWEE-XEEN,	he growls,
LUK-KWEE-XEEN	he growls

For enjoyment, Lenape families would dance around fires at night and sing chants.

PSALM 23

The Lord is my Shepherd; I shall
   not want.

He makes me lie down in green
   pastures;
he leads me beside still waters;
   he restores my soul.
He leads me in right paths
   for his name's sake.

Even though I walk through the
   darkest valley,
   I fear no evil;
for you are with me;
   your rod and your staff —
   they comfort me.

Quaker families recited psalms from the Bible for comfort and to reaffirm their beliefs.

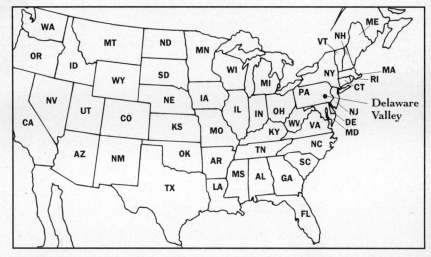

Modern map of the continental United States, showing the approximate location of the Delaware Valley in Pennsylvania.

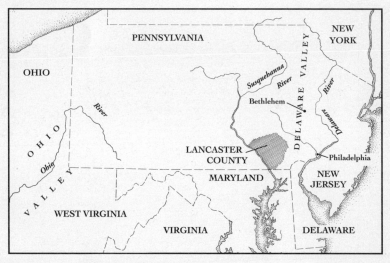

This map of the Delaware Valley and surrounding areas shows places mentioned in the diary.

About the Author

MARY POPE OSBORNE has long had an interest in American history. She has published biographies of George Washington and Benjamin Franklin, as well as a collection of American tall tales. Her interest in the Lenape Indians began ten years ago when she and her husband, Will, bought a summer cabin in the woods of the Delaware Valley of Pennsylvania. Her knowledge of the area, combined with a fascination with Indian captive narratives and a deep respect for the Quaker faith, led her to develop the story that became Catharine's diary.

"In the autumn, while writing in our cabin, on land where Catharine's farm might have been, I felt as if I were living in a sort of dream time. At midnight, listening to the leaves rattling in the wind, I felt Catharine's fear as she anticipated the Indians' attack. Canoeing on our creek, I was Catharine traveling to the Lenape camp. Walking near a cornfield on a cool, sunny day, I imagined the moment when the soldiers crashed through the corn rows. I attended meetings at an historic Quaker meetinghouse nearby. I roamed the site of a Lenape village. My own experiences in the Delaware Valley made Catharine's life feel immediate and alive to me."

Mary Pope Osborne is the award-winning author of more than forty books for children, among them the best-selling *Magic Tree House* series; *One World, Many Religions,* a 1997 Orbis Pictus Honor Book; and four books of classic stories from around the world, including, *Favorite Medieval Tales,* published by Scholastic Press. She has just completed two terms as president of the Authors Guild, the leading authors' organization in America.

Acknowledgments

The author would like to thank The Museum of the American Indian in New York City; The Mercer Museum in Doylestown, Pennsylvania; The Quaker Meetinghouse in Quakertown, Pennsylvania; and The Churchville Nature Center in Churchville, Pennsylvania. She would also like to thank Tracy Mack for her wonderful editing, Marge Custer at The Churchville Nature Center, Sheila Kogan, Diane Nesin, and Melissa Jenkins.

Page 169 (right): Lenape woman, ibid.

Page 170: Farm scene, The Library of Congress

Page 171: *Geography in an Early Friends School*, drawing by J. Walter West.

Page 172 (top): Friend's Bank Meeting House, The Library Company of Philadelphia, Philadelphia, Pennsylvania.

Page 172 (bottom): William Penn meeting with the colonists, Library of Congress

Page 173 (top): Deed from Delaware Indians to William Penn, The Historical Society of Pennsylvania, Philadelphia, Pennsylvania.

Page 173 (bottom): *Penn's Treaty with the Indians*, painting by Benjamin West. Courtesy of the Pennsylvania Academy of Fine Arts, Philadelphia, Pennsylvania. Gift of Mrs. Sarah Harrison (The Joseph Harrison Jr. Collection).

Page 174: Portrait of La-Pa-Win-Soe, Library of Congress

Page 175 (top): Building of longhouse, drawing by Dr. Herbert Kraft, Seton Hall University, South Orange, New Jersey.

Page 175 (bottom): Interior of longhouse, ibid.

Page 176 (top): Lenape women in garden, ibid.

Page 176 (bottom): Canoe building, ibid.

Page 177: Captive narrative, The Library of Congress

Page 178: Returning the captives, ibid.

Page 180 (top): Lenape chant, The Churchville Nature Center, Churchville, Pennsylvania.

Page 181: Maps by Heather Saunders

Other books in the Dear America series

A Journey to the New World
The Diary of Remember Patience Whipple
by Kathryn Lasky

The Winter of Red Snow
The Revolutionary War Diary of Abigail Jane Stewart
by Kristiana Gregory

When Will This Cruel War Be Over?
The Civil War Diary of Emma Simpson
by Barry Denenberg

A Picture of Freedom
The Diary of Clotee, a Slave Girl
by Patricia C. McKissack

Across the Wide and Lonesome Prairie
The Oregon Trail Diary of Hattie Campbell
by Kristiana Gregory

So Far from Home
The Diary of Mary Driscoll, an Irish Mill Girl
by Barry Denenberg

I Thought My Soul Would Rise and Fly
The Diary of Patsy, a Freed Girl
by Joyce Hansen

West to a Land of Plenty
The Diary of Teresa Angelino Viscardi
by Jim Murphy

Dreams in the Golden Country
The Diary of Zipporah Feldman, a Jewish Immigrant Girl
by Kathryn Lasky

A Line in the Sand
The Alamo Diary of Lucinda Lawrence
by Sherry Garland

Voyage on the Great Titanic
The Diary of Margaret Ann Brady
by Ellen Emerson White

For my mother

Copyright © 1998 by Mary Pope Osborne.

All rights reserved. Published by Scholastic Inc.
557 Broadway, New York, New York 10012.
DEAR AMERICA®, SCHOLASTIC, and associated logos
are trademarks and/or registered trademarks of Scholastic Inc.

Library of Congress Cataloging-in-Publication Data available.

ISBN 0-590-13462-0;
ISBN 0-439-44554-X (pbk.)

10 9 8 7 6 5 4 3 2   02 03 04 05 06

The display type was set in Novella Bold.
The text type was set in Cochin.
Book design by Elizabeth B. Parisi

Printed in the U.S.A. 23
First paperback printing, October 2002